Charlie looked at the woman who was sitting opposite him, taking notes.

She wasn't the Ellie Newton he'd known ten years ago, the shy girl who kept to herself at school. She'd even changed her name to Elle—sophisticated and glamorous, to match the way she looked. Though he couldn't think of her as anyone other than Ellie.

Right now, she looked like all the women in his old life, wearing a smart office dress, high heels and her dark hair in a high-maintenance pixie cut. Her nails were perfectly manicured, her makeup flawless—and the bright red lipstick she wore made him very aware of the curve of her mouth. For a mad second, he found himself wondering what it would be like to feel that mouth against his own, sweet and teasing and utterly seductive...

But that wasn't going to happen.

Apart from the fact he wasn't in the market for any kind of relationship—it would feel like a betrayal of Jess—this meeting was all about business.

Dear Reader,

Fake fiancé is my absolute favourite trope—so I've been a little bit indulgent with both the subject and the setting in my one hundredth title. It's set in the bit of the world where I live, complete with bluebell woods, and there's a scene at the beach where my husband took me on our first Saturday date.

So we have marketing guru Elle, who's convinced she's a city girl and avoids the farm where she grew up, and Charlie, widowed tragically early in London and who's gone from a banker to an ecologist, turning Elle's family farm into a rare breeds/ rewilding sanctuary.

When Elle nearly loses her job and her boss gives her a month to learn how to be family oriented, she asks Charlie to be her fake fiancé on social media in return for sorting out the farm's marketing. Knowing they want completely different things out of life, they think they're safe from falling for each other—but their hearts have other ideas!

Can they find a compromise? Read on to find out!

With love—and thank you for being with me on this journey to one hundred books.

Kate Hardy

Tempted by Her Fake Fiancé

—

Kate Hardy

Recycling programs
for this product may
not exist in your area.

ISBN-13: 978-1-335-73700-7

Tempted by Her Fake Fiancé

Copyright © 2023 by Pamela Brooks

For questions and comments about the quality of this book, please contact us at CustomerService@Harlequin.com.

Harlequin Enterprises ULC
22 Adelaide St. West, 41st Floor
Toronto, Ontario M5H 4E3, Canada
www.Harlequin.com

Printed in U.S.A.

Kate Hardy has been a bookworm since she was a toddler. When she isn't writing, Kate enjoys reading, theatre, live music, ballet and the gym. She lives with her husband, student children and their spaniel in Norwich, England. You can contact her via her website, katehardy.com.

Books by Kate Hardy

Harlequin Romance

A Crown by Christmas

Soldier Prince's Secret Baby Gift

Summer at Villa Rosa

The Runaway Bride and the Billionaire

Reunited at the Altar
A Diamond in the Snow
Finding Mr. Right in Florence
One Night to Remember
A Will, a Wish, a Wedding
Surprise Heir for the Princess
Snowbound with the Millionaire
One Week in Venice with the CEO
Crowning His Secret Princess

Visit the Author Profile page
at Harlequin.com for more titles.

To my family, friends, readers and editors who've been with me on the journey to my one hundredth Harlequin book—thank you. I couldn't have done it without you! Xx

CHAPTER ONE

'ELLE, YOU'RE GOOD with shoestring budgets,' Rav said. 'I've got a project I want you to handle.'

Even though Elle had a ridiculous workload at the moment—because she'd been pushing herself harder ever since the head of the agency had announced a restructure that would mean a new senior account manager, a job she really wanted—she smiled at her boss. 'Sure. Do we have a brief and a pitch meeting scheduled?'

'Not *quite*,' Rav said. 'The client's already seen your work and liked it. He happened to be in London this morning, so he wanted to meet you and talk over the brief for the marketing campaign himself.'

'That's fine.' If she worked through lunch—*again*—she'd be able to juggle her deadlines; Elle was pretty sure she could carve out enough time to get herself up to speed on the client's current marketing and his competitors before the meeting. 'What time's he coming in?'

Rav coughed. 'He's waiting in the meeting room, right now.'

Oh. So she wasn't even going to have time to check out the client's website, let alone come up with any ideas. 'Just as well I can think on my feet,' she said dryly.

'It's a skill we're looking for in the new senior account manager,' Rav said.

Her heart skipped a beat. Was her boss hinting…?

'Hugo's delighted with what you've been doing lately,' Rav said. Hugo, the head of the agency, was notoriously difficult to please. He could spot the most minor fault at a thousand paces, and his door-slamming abilities were legendary. 'We were talking about the restructure yesterday, and whether we should recruit internally or externally. We're both of the same mind. Get this campaign going viral, Elle,' Rav added, 'and the senior account manager job's yours.'

That wasn't a hint: it was explicit. All the hours she'd put in were finally going to pay off, provided she got the campaign to go viral; and Elle intended to pull out all the stops to make absolutely sure it did. 'Thank you, Rav,' she said quietly.

'I'll take you in to meet the client,' Rav said.

But no introductions were necessary.

The second Elle walked into the room, she

recognised the man sitting at the table. Charlie Webb's stunning blue eyes were unmistakable: the colour, she thought, of the bluebells in the wood at the edge of her family farm. Despite the fact that he was wearing a business suit, he looked more like the presenter of a TV nature programme, with his dark hair brushed back from his forehead. The tan he'd got from working outside really suited him, and she'd just bet that the expensive material of his suit hid some serious muscles.

She damped down the little frisson of attraction that bubbled through her. Charlie Webb was completely off limits. Apart from the fact that he was her dad's business partner, when they'd last met she'd sobbed her heart out on Charlie's shoulder. Prom night, ten years ago, had possibly been the worst episode in her time at high school.

Not that it was relevant now. She'd moved on from the unhappy, bullied teenager she'd been back then, reinventing herself as hotshot marketer Elle Newton. She fitted in with her colleagues, the way she'd never been able to fit in at school, and she knew she was good at what she did.

'Good morning, Charlie,' she said brightly.

'Hello, Ellie,' he said.

Of course he'd use her old name. Her parents did, too, though she didn't quite have the heart to correct them: because that would lead to too many questions she didn't want to answer. Instead, she gave him a polite smile. 'Actually, nowadays I go by Elle.'

'You two know each other?' Rav asked, looking surprised.

For a moment, adrenaline pumped through Elle's veins. How much was Charlie going to divulge? The last thing she wanted was her life in London colliding with her old, hated life in Norfolk.

'Yes. Ellie—Elle,' Charlie corrected himself, 'was in the same year at school as my little sister.'

Elle had to stop herself from physically sagging with relief, but inwardly she still felt like a half-set jelly. This was too close for comfort. She didn't want her boss to see the vulnerable girl she'd once been; she needed him to keep seeing her as she was now. Confident and capable. The woman who'd make a great senior account manager.

Rav looked delighted. 'As I don't need to introduce you, I'll leave you to it.'

Elle waited until Rav had closed the door behind him. 'Rav said you wanted us to work on a marketing campaign for you, because you've seen my work and liked it.' But why on earth would Bluebell Farm need a London marketing agency's help? Had Charlie got another job and left her parents in the lurch? She took a breath. Jumping to conclusions would be the quickest way to lose this brief—and her promotion. 'I assume,' she said, careful to sound neutral rather than judgmental, 'that you're leaving the farm and you're here for something to do with a new venture?'

'No,' he said. 'I'm here for Bluebell Farm.'

She sat down, frowning. 'Sorry, Charlie, but I don't quite understand.'

'I've managed the farm for the last two years,' Charlie said.

'I know.' And she still felt guilty about it. The job she knew her dad had always wanted her to do: take over Bluebell Farm and manage it until she was ready to hand it over to the next generation. A job she couldn't bear even to think about, much less actually do. She knew her dad had reached the age when the super-early mornings were getting a bit too much for him: the endless grind of milking twice a day, making sure there was clean water in the troughs, feeding the cows, checking the fences, keeping a check on the herd's health, mucking out in winter when the cows were sleeping in the barn overnight, worrying about the weather and how it would affect the grain crops...

She also knew that two years ago she should've

offered to give up her life in London and go home: but she simply couldn't force the words out of her mouth. As a child, she'd loved the farm; as a teen, she'd grown to hate it. Her association with the farm had made her life at high school utterly miserable. The popular crowd had called her 'Smelly Ellie' from her first day at high school, claiming that she smelled of cows—even though she knew she didn't, because she'd always showered after milking and before she went to school, and she also used copious amounts of body spray to mask any lingering bovine residue. The bullies had gleefully homed in on her insecurity; it was made worse by the fact that 'new' in the local accent was pronounced 'noo', and it was an easy step from there to 'moo'. *Smelly Ellie Moo-ton. Hurgh, hurgh, hurgh.* They'd been so pleased by their wit. *Got a face on her like sour milk, geddit?*

Even the ones who weren't part of the popular set had joined in, grateful that they weren't the ones on the receiving end of the constant teasing and sniping. It hadn't helped that Elle had been plump as a teenager, despite the physical work she did on the farm; if they weren't calling her *Moo-ton* it was *Heifer*.

She'd vowed not to set foot in the place any more often than she had to, once she'd escaped to London. At eighteen, she'd reinvented herself as Elle Newton, worked hard at university, made her mark with internships during the university holidays, and ended up with a glittering career in a high-profile industry. She loved London, she loved her job, and she loved her life here. And she'd been really relieved two years ago when her dad had suggested hiring Charlie—who'd just finished his MSc, after doing a project on the farm—as his new farm manager.

'Do Mum and Dad know you're here?' she asked.

'Of course. We've been talking about the marketing for the farm, and they agreed you were the obvious choice for the job.'

And that was the bit that really flummoxed her. 'Charlie, I really don't get it. Why does Bluebell Farm need a London marketing agency?'

'Because we're moving things forward.' He paused. 'As you'd have seen for yourself, if you ever came back to the farm.'

He'd hit the bullseye of her guilt. Not that she was going to let him know it. 'My life's in London, now, not West Byfield.' The back of beyond: a small market town in Norfolk where everyone knew everything about everyone else, mobile phone coverage was still spotty, broadband speeds meant you were two seconds behind everyone else on a video-call, and there were four buses a day to Norwich and none at all on Sundays. If she went back now, it'd be like being in the same glass box as her teen years, unable to join in and knowing that everyone was mocking her.

Absolutely no way.

Even though Charlie was being a bit judgemental right now—a far cry from the nice guy who'd rescued her, that horrible night—having a fight with him wasn't going to help this project. She'd worked hard for a promotion; this project was going to clinch it for her, and she had no intention of losing out. Which meant being her professional self and unruffling his feathers, rather than escalating the argument. She gave him her best professional smile and said, 'Tell me about the project.'

'We're rewilding the farm,' he said.

'Dad said you've switched from dairy farming to raising rare breeds.'

'There's no money in dairy farming,' Charlie said. 'It's at the point where it costs more to produce the milk than the customer pays for it. A developer offered to buy your dad out, last year, but he refused.'

That was something her dad hadn't mentioned to her, but Elle pushed down the sting of hurt. She could hardly complain about being shut out from anything farm-related when she'd been the one to walk away. 'Accepting an offer like that would've meant he could retire,' she said.

'What, and see a massive housing estate built on the land his family had farmed for generations?' Charlie asked, his tone deceptively mild.

If he could play the guilt card, so could she. 'It could've been affordable housing for local people,' she countered.

Charlie shook his head. 'That's not what those developers were about. And their plans were the complete opposite of what we're doing.'

'So there's money in rare breeds?'

'It's important,' he said.

In other words, there wasn't any money in rare breeds, either.

She knew Charlie had bought into the farm a few months ago; was his money financing the rewilding and keeping the farm afloat? she wondered. And what would happen to Bluebell Farm when his money ran out?

'Conservation saves species from extinction and preserves heritage,' he said.

'What sort of species?' she asked.

'We have a small herd of British White cows, a small flock of Norfolk Horn sheep, a flock of Norfolk Grey chickens and a couple of goats,' he said. 'We might be getting a Suffolk Punch and a donkey, in a couple of weeks.'

Donkeys definitely weren't rare breeds. 'Surely farming rare breeds is an expensive hobby rather than a money-making business,' she said.

'Not necessarily. This is where you come in,' he said. 'We want to raise the profile of the rare breeds and the rewilding project. The farm also needs to support itself a bit better, so we also need to raise awareness of what we offer.'

'Which is?'

'School visits, a farm café and shop, guided nature walks, a few relevant classes—we have an art teacher and a photography teacher, and a woman who runs spinning classes.'

For a mad moment, Elle had a vision of a barn full of exercise cycles, with an instructor at the front encouraging clients to pedal harder. But of *course* Charlie meant spinning as in wool, not spinning as in one of her usual gym classes. 'Right,' she said.

'We have holiday accommodation,' he said, 'and people can choose to help with the rewilding project and the animals, or just use it as a base for exploring the area.'

'You've converted some of the barns for the accommodation?' she asked.

'No. There are the two farm cottages—I live in the third—plus I bought three shepherd's huts. Purpose-built luxury boutique huts with a comfortable bed, a decent shower and a kitchen, and a private space for sitting out with a wood-fired hot tub. They're available for stays of two nights or more.'

No more large dairy herd. No more living in muddy wellies and sludge-coloured boiler suits. No more harvesting at all hours in the summer when the weather was right and the corn was ripe; Elle remembered taking dinner out to her dad in a box because he refused to come indoors until the light was too poor for him to work. It was how things had been for her entire life, and she couldn't quite get her head round the idea of the farm being so different, now.

'Got it,' she fibbed. 'So it's education and re-wilding plus glamping and the shop and café, basically.'

'We're also planning to start hosting weddings; we've already got the licence, so we were thinking of holding the ceremony itself at one end of the largest barn, and the wedding breakfast and dancing at the other end.'

'Four different audiences, then. OK.'

Charlie looked at the woman who was sitting opposite him, taking notes. She wasn't the Ellie Newton he'd known ten years ago. The shy girl who kept herself to herself at school because the popular kids jeered at her; the teenager who'd sobbed on his shoulder when she'd literally run into him and he'd taken her to one side, thinking how easily it could've been his sister fleeing from the prom in tears. She'd even changed her name to Elle—sophisticated and glamorous, to match the way she looked. Though he couldn't think of her as anyone other than Ellie.

Right now, she looked like all the women in his old life: wearing a smart office dress, high heels, and with her long dark hair shot through with chestnut highlights. Her nails were perfectly manicured, her make-up flawless—and the bright red lipstick she wore made him very aware of the curve of her mouth. For a mad second, he found himself wondering what it would be like to feel that mouth against his own, sweet and teasing and utterly seductive...

But that wasn't going to happen.

Apart from the fact he wasn't in the market for any kind of relationship—it would still feel like a betrayal of Jess—this meeting was all about business.

Elle Newton had won awards for her work; he knew she'd do an excellent job at raising the farm's profile. Particularly because she'd have a personal stake in it, with Bluebell Farm being her family's business. Or, rather, since he'd bought into it six months ago, almost *half* her family's business.

'I only knew about this meeting about three minutes before I walked in the door,' she said, 'so unfortunately I haven't had time to look at the farm's website or look at what your competitors are doing, and that means I'm working blind. Usually clients book a meeting in advance, giving us a brief, so we can at least do some preliminary work.'

He noted the rebuke, even though it had been polite. 'I happened to be in London for the weekend—a former colleague's retirement do,' he said. 'And it occurred to me that I could drop in this morning and see if Hugo could squeeze me in. If it hadn't been possible, I would've sent in a brief and booked a meeting later.'

Her eyes narrowed. 'Hang on. You're on first-name terms with the head of the agency?'

'He used to play golf with my old boss. I've met him a few times at various functions,' Charlie said.

'So does he know that you work with my dad?'

Charlie didn't understand the momentary expression of wariness on her face, even though it was quickly hidden. 'I wasn't explicit about the connection. I said I'd seen your work and liked it, and I thought you'd be the right one to handle the project.'

'Right.' She was definitely in cool mode now,

and Charlie didn't have a clue what he'd done or said to upset her.

'Let's start from the basics. Does Bluebell Farm actually have a website?' she asked.

'Yes.'

'And people can book the accommodation through it?'

'No. They phone us,' he said.

She made a note. 'What about the café and farm shop? Can people book a table through the website, or buy things online?'

'We don't do bookings and we don't have an online shop,' he said. 'We book the school visits in advance, but again they phone us to arrange it.'

'How about a blog? Or any kind of social media?'

'There isn't really any time to handle that,' he said.

'OK. So it sounds as if we're looking at a website revamp and a media plan,' she said. 'Social media, article placement, advertising—'

'We don't have a huge budget,' he cut in.

'I was hardly going to suggest a campaign with primetime TV,' she said, rolling her eyes. 'Actually, now you've mentioned the budget: why didn't Mum and Dad ask me to do this for them in my spare time? They must know I would have done it for them for nothing rather than them having to pay London agency fees.'

He lifted one shoulder. 'Maybe they thought you'd be too busy.'

Her eyes narrowed. 'I'm never too busy for my parents.'

But she never came back to West Byfield. He'd noticed that, over the last two and a half years. Mike and Angie always visited their daughter in London rather than the other way round. They came back bubbling about what a lovely time they'd spent with her, the way she'd surprised them with a show or dinner out and made a huge fuss of them: but it was very obvious to him that Ellie Newton was avoiding Bluebell Farm. He knew that she'd been unhappy in West Byfield, as a teen, but surely she'd moved on from that misery over the last ten years?

'Besides, this isn't about your parents. This is part of my investment,' he said. 'I assume you know I have a forty per cent stake in the farm.'

'Dad mentioned it, yes.'

Was she angry, relieved, or worried about it? He didn't have a clue. She was all cool professionalism, betraying no trace of her feelings. That felt strange; he was used to being able to read people well. Elle Newton was an enigma. She intrigued him, and that made him antsy. He didn't want to feel that spark of interest in anyone.

'We were talking about what you expect from

the agency,' she continued. 'Word-of-mouth customer referrals are the best kind, but you need to support that. You need people to know where you are and what you can offer them. That means sending press releases to targeted media about weddings, holidays and ecology; and making sure you have a solid website, so if customers leave a review on any of the tourist websites, then other potential customers can click on the link and take a look at what you're offering.'

'Which is where you come in.'

She nodded. 'I'll need to do a SWOT analysis and look at your USPs—that's jargon for looking at what you're good at and how to maximise it, what you need to improve, what your competition is doing and the differences between that and what you offer. Give me the rest of the day to have a look at where you are now and where you need to be, then maybe we can set up a video-call meeting tomorrow for me to grill you about the rest of it.'

'It's probably easier,' he said, knowing perfectly well that he was practically lobbing a grenade at her, 'if you come back to the farm to see it for yourself.'

Go back to the farm.

It was the last thing Elle wanted to do.

On the other hand, if she refused, it meant that someone else would take over the project, and she didn't want that either. It shocked her to realise that she actually felt protective about the farm; or maybe it was her parents she felt protective about. Even if whoever handled the project in her agency dealt with Charlie, she didn't want anyone else dealing with her parents and maybe judging them the way that the cool kids at school had judged her.

And if her colleagues found out about her background...

It wasn't that she was ashamed of where she came from; it was more that she hated the way other people reacted to it. It hadn't been just the popular kids at school who'd given her a hard time about the farm; her boyfriends at university had behaved in pretty much the same way, once she'd taken them back to West Byfield. OK, so she had rubbish taste in men—what had happened with Damien Price at prom should've warned her about that—but it had squashed her heart a little bit flatter every time she brought someone to the farm to meet her parents, and they dumped her shortly afterwards. *'It's not you, it's me...'* She'd heard it too many times, and she'd known it hadn't been the truth. It had been Bluebell Farm. Her boyfriends had been put off by the cows and the mud and the shabbiness.

She didn't want any of it affecting her life in London now; but she didn't want to let her parents down, either. There had to be a middle way.

'I'm really not sure I can spare the time to come to Norfolk,' she said. 'It'd be much quicker to do it all by video call.'

'I'm sure your boss would let you have a few days,' Charlie said. 'Maybe even a couple of weeks, so you can wrap it all up on site.'

'A couple of weeks?' She winced inwardly, hearing the squeak of panic in her voice. 'Sorry. That's completely out of the question. And I never spend two whole weeks doing a client visit—even if they have a massive budget.'

'You said you would've done it for nothing, in your spare time,' Charlie said. 'Can I be cheeky and ask if you could maybe take some holiday?'

A working holiday in the place she'd been desperate to escape from ten years ago?

It was very far from Elle's idea of fun. She had no problems with the concept of a working holiday; it was the destination that rattled her.

'You could stay in one of the shepherd's huts and experience things on the farm, the way our visitors would. It would give you the perfect insight,' he said.

Back to Bluebell Farm.

It felt as if someone had just draped a blanket of lead round her shoulders: all the misery of her teenage years, solidified and weighing her down again.

'I do have other clients. Not to mention deadlines,' she said.

'Your mum said you haven't taken any time off in six months. I'm surprised the HR department hasn't been on your case about it,' he said.

Was this an oblique way of telling her that she needed to go back for a different reason— perhaps that one of her parents was seriously ill but hadn't told her because they didn't want her to worry? 'Are Mum and Dad all right?' she asked. 'There isn't something they're...' Anxiety made her spine prickle and she dragged in a breath. 'Something they're not telling me?'

'They're fine. Why would you...?' He frowned, then grimaced. 'Sorry. I didn't mean to scare you, or make you think there was an ulterior motive for asking you to come back. Your parents are both fine. It's just that I think you'll get a better feel for what we're doing if you come and see it for yourself.'

It was true. With any other client, she'd do a site visit, because it meant she'd come in as a fresh pair of eyes and be able to see things that maybe the client took for granted or hadn't really thought about.

But this was Bluebell Farm. Her unhappy place. Something she'd rather do at a distance.

'I'll need to ask my boss,' she said. She was pretty sure she could couch the request in a way that would make him say no. 'If I can't take the time off, then we'll have to do a video conference instead.'

He frowned. 'I can't take you on a live video tour of the farm.'

She knew why. 'Because of all the Wi-Fi dead spots.'

'But that's part of the charm for people who want to have a complete break.' He smiled. 'Spotty mobile phone coverage means you might as well switch off your phone completely.'

'That's meant to be a selling point?' she scoffed. 'A deal-breaker, more like, in today's world.'

'It's definitely a selling point,' he said. He looked at her. 'Ellie, the farm needs help. It needs you. Your mum and dad need you.'

'That,' she said, 'is emotional blackmail. If you were talking to anyone else in the agency, you wouldn't be saying it.'

'No. But we want you to handle the project,' he said. 'You're good at this. Your mum's got a photograph on the mantelpiece of you accepting your last award, right next to your graduation photo.'

'More emotional blackmail,' she said, folding her arms.

'OK, I get that you don't want to come back to the farm,' he said. 'But we still need help. If you'd rather not do it, then OK: we'll just have to find someone else. You were the first choice because of your parents, and because their share of the farm will be yours one day—I think you ought to have some input into what we're doing, rather than leave it to someone else.'

'I'm not part of the business, and I'll support my parents' choices,' she said, narrowing her eyes at him.

Why had Charlie Webb had to walk into her agency and turn her life upside down?

If she agreed to help, she'd hate every minute she spent at the farm. If she refused to do it, she'd feel as if she was letting her parents down. Whatever she did, she lost.

There wasn't a middle way. She'd have to choose the lesser of two evils. 'If I can get the time off,' she said, 'I'll do it.'

'Great.' He looked pleased. 'I can give you a lift back today.'

'Hang on. I can't just drop everything,' she said. 'I have commitments and there are things I'll need to move. Let me talk to my boss, and I'll call you later.'

'All right.' He handed her a business card. 'If

I'm in a dead spot, my phone will go through to voicemail. Leave me a message and I'll call you back.'

'I'll look over the website later today,' she said, 'and I'll have a list of questions and suggestions.'

'Great.' He stood up and held out his hand. 'Thanks for your time, Ellie. *Elle*,' he corrected himself swiftly.

Shaking his hand was meant to feel like a normal business gesture, but Elle's skin tingled where it touched his. She didn't dare look him in the eye, in case he guessed.

Charlie Webb was her client, she reminded herself. Blurring the boundaries of that relationship would affect her job, and that in turn would mean she'd miss out on the promotion she'd worked so hard for. Not going to happen. Even if that hadn't been a barrier, she wasn't looking for a relationship. She'd given up on trying to find Mr Right and she was totally focused on her career.

'Nice to see you again, Charlie,' she said, giving him her most professional smile.

Once she'd shown him out to Reception, Elle took a quick break to video-call her mum and check that her parents really were on board with what Charlie was doing with the farm. A phone call wasn't good enough; she needed to look into her mum's eyes and be sure that Angie Newton was telling her the truth. 'He's not pushing you into things, Mum, is he?'

'No, love. Actually, his energy's refreshing,' Angie said. 'I was a bit surprised when he, of all people, suggested we start doing weddings, but he's got a point. This is a beautiful part of the world to be married in. And if people want to marry in the local church, he's planning to offer a horse and carriage to transport the bride and groom between here and the church.'

'What do you mean, you were surprised when he suggested weddings?' Elle asked.

'I thought you knew.'

Elle frowned. 'Knew what?'

Angie looked awkward. 'Oh, love. I don't want to gossip. Maybe you should ask him.'

This sounded like something important. 'Mum, please, just tell me,' Elle said. 'I know you're not a gossip and you know I'm not, either. This sounds like something I need to be aware of, so I don't accidentally put my foot in it.'

'His wife was killed in an accident, hit by a car.'

God, he was young to be a widower, Elle thought. Thirty-one: only three years older than herself. 'That's tough. Poor Charlie.'

'He couldn't bear to stay in London after she died. That's why he gave up his job in the City

and went to do his Masters in Environmental
Studies, and he ended up doing his final project
here. Your dad liked his ideas, and that's why
he offered Charlie a job to manage the farm and
do the rewilding.'

And Charlie's successful career in the City
would've given him the cash to buy that chunky
share of the farm a few months ago, Elle
thought. 'When did she die?'

'Five years ago,' Angie said. 'He's barely
dated since. I know Barb—' his mother, and
one of Angie's friends even though she'd moved
away '—worries herself sick about him.'

Elle took the rest of the comment as read:
Angie was just as worried about her singleton
daughter. 'Thanks for telling me, Mum. I'll
tread carefully.'

'You're really coming back to the farm?' Angie's face brightened.

'If I can get my boss to agree, I'll stay for a
few days,' Elle said. 'To sort out everything for
the media project.'

'I can't wait to see you, love.'

Guilt flooded through Elle. She loved her parents dearly, and she knew that a thrice-weekly
video call and the treats she sent them really
weren't enough. But forcing herself to go back
to the farm was like taking off a plaster very,
very slowly. 'And you, Mum. I'd better go. But

I just wanted to be sure you and Dad weren't being steamrollered before I started putting things in place at this end.'

'Charlie's a nice boy,' Angie said. 'He's kind.'

Yeah. But Elle couldn't tell her mother how she already knew that. It would involve explanations that would hurt her parents, and that wasn't fair. 'I'll see you soon. Love you.'

She went to see Rav and closed his office door behind her. 'Can we have a confidential word, please?' she asked.

'Of course.' Rav looked concerned. 'Is something wrong?'

She took a deep breath. 'In the interests of full disclosure—and also in strictest confidence—I need to tell you that Bluebell Farm belongs to my parents as well as to Charlie Webb.'

'Your parents?' He blinked. 'So you already know all about what they want?'

'No.' At his surprised stare, she hedged, 'It's…complicated.'

'Is it a problem?'

It could be. But Rav had asked her to do the project, and been explicit about promoting her if she did a good job. She'd make sure it didn't become a problem. 'No. I was just a bit surprised, because I didn't realise they were changing things quite so much, to the point where they do actually need a marketing plan.' She didn't want to bring up all the mud and the manure. Or her own ambivalence towards the farm. 'They want me to go and stay for a few days. I know a site visit wouldn't normally take more than a day, and I know this is ridiculously short notice, but...' She bit her lip. 'Would it be possible for me to go tomorrow, and take a few days' holiday to do it?'

'In other words, you're planning to work through your holiday to keep their budget low? HR would have my head on a platter for even entertaining the idea,' Rav said, shaking his head.

'Two weeks. One day as work, the rest as holiday,' Elle said.

'When you'll still be working.'

She squirmed. 'Look, I don't want anyone else to do it, because this is my family we're talking about and I want to support them. As long as that's not a problem for you?'

'If anything,' Rav said, 'it means you've got an even stronger motivation to make this campaign succeed.'

'I do. And it's a shoestring budget, so I think this is the best solution,' she said. 'This is my family, so I admit I plan to do some of the work in my own time. But, as far as HR is concerned, I'm on holiday.'

'And you think that's acceptable, not having a proper break?' Rav asked dryly.

'We all have to put in extra hours sometimes, to make things work,' she said. 'I wouldn't do it for any other client. This is my family. You'd do the same, wouldn't you, if it was your family's business?'

Rav looked at her for a long, long moment. 'Yes. I know where you're coming from.'

'Good. There shouldn't be a problem on any of my projects. I'm up to date with everything, and all the dates, deadlines and details for the next steps are in my project plans.'

'I wouldn't expect anything else from the queen of critical path analysis.' Rav inclined his head. 'All right. I'll let HR know. Actually, they did bring your name up this morning as someone who hasn't taken time off for a while and they're a bit antsy about it, so I'm sure we can live with the short notice of your "holiday". Though I do expect you to take a bit of a break while you're away.'

'I will. There won't be any commuting, for a start.' She gave him what she hoped was a winning smile.

He rolled his eyes. 'Go and hand over your projects, then do whatever you need to make that campaign go viral. But I meant it about a break. I want you refreshed when you come back to London, not worn out.'

'Thanks, Rav.'

Elle messaged her parents to say that she'd be at the farm in the morning, and Charlie to say that she'd be getting the seven a.m. train from Liverpool Street to Norwich tomorrow and then grabbing a taxi; then she spent the rest of the day sorting out last-minute issues and handing over her projects to colleagues. Back at her flat, she cancelled her next two weeks of classes at the gym and booked her train ticket, rang her best friend to let her know what was going on and that she needed to cancel drinks and their film night for the next two Thursdays, then settled down to look through Bluebell Farm's website and social media accounts.

Home-made websites could be charming; Bluebell Farm's wasn't. It was muddled and didn't give anywhere near enough information. No wonder the farm wasn't paying for itself.

Well, that was where she came in.

Elle had just finished some notes and was starting to look up farm holidays and weddings, when her phone beeped with a couple of texts. The first was from Charlie, to say he'd meet her at the station. The second was from her dad, to say he was delighted that she was coming to help.

She tried to brush off the flurry of guilt. Right now, she still wasn't entirely sure that this was the best idea. She was filled with a mixture of trepidation at going back to the place where she'd been so unhappy, worry about setting up expectations with her parents that she'd never be able to fulfil, and very muddled-up feelings about Charlie Webb—who'd definitely got hotter over the past ten years. She'd noticed how many women walking through Reception had given him a second look. If she hadn't known him, she would've given him a second look, herself: probably a third.

But his past would put another barrier between them; her mum had said that he wasn't dating, so clearly he wasn't ready to move on after his wife's tragic death. This was going to be strictly business. She'd do the job as professionally as she could, and then she'd come back to London. Get her promotion. And then she could settle down to the lovely, full life she'd worked for—far away from Bluebell Farm.

CHAPTER TWO

CHARLIE HAD COMPLETELY miscalculated how long it would take him to drive through rush-hour traffic. He rarely came into the city, and he hadn't even considered how many sets of roadworks and diversions there might be on the arterial roads. Add frustrated commuters trying to get to work on time, people on e-scooters weaving rashly in and out of the traffic and even driving the wrong way down the road…

At least his car had hands-free connection to his phone, so he was able to text Ellie and let her know he'd be a bit late picking her up at the train station.

Ellie Newton.

Funny how the ends of his fingers were tingling with adrenaline at the idea of seeing her again.

Ten years ago, he'd seen her practically as a child. Eighteen, the same age as his little sister. Completely off limits. Now, she was all grown up. The prodigal daughter, coming home. Except she'd made it clear that she didn't want to be there. He was pretty sure there wasn't a rift between Ellie and her parents; he ate dinner with Mike and Angie in their kitchen, a couple of times a week, and he knew from chatting with them that she called them often and sent them little surprises. So what kept her away from them?

He knew why he avoided his own parents and was glad they'd moved away to be nearer his sister; he loved them, but he simply couldn't cope with their pity and their attempts at finding someone to take Jess's place in his life. He avoided his in-laws and Jess's friends because he couldn't handle the weight of their grief on top of his own; and his friends and former colleagues just didn't know what to say to him, so the gaps between phone calls and promises to meet up soon had grown longer and longer, until eventually he couldn't remember the last time he'd even spoken to one of them, let alone seen them. The only one of his family who didn't make him feel worse, or try to set him up with 'someone suitable who'll heal your heart again', was his little sister, Jo—and he was pretty sure that was only because right now she was busy with a toddler and a new baby.

Mike and Angie Newton had given him

space to grieve and space to breathe. Working on Bluebell Farm, both during his MSc project and since they'd offered him a job afterwards, had gone a long way to mending the broken bits inside him. He couldn't understand why Ellie didn't want to be here, with a family who loved her. London was glittery and busy and noisy, yes, but after Jess's death he'd found his life there shallow and empty. It wasn't a boyfriend keeping Ellie in London, either, because Charlie had picked up from several conversations that Angie and Mike worried she'd never settle down.

Ellie the enigma.

He wanted to know what made her tick.

Though he had a feeling that she might have as many barriers around her as he did.

She was waiting for him at the station entrance, concentrating on her phone; he pressed the button to lower the passenger window and called her name.

She looked up and smiled, and it felt as if all the breath had just gone out of his lungs. Dressed much more casually than yesterday, in jeans, a pale yellow T-shirt, canvas shoes and no make-up, she was absolutely gorgeous.

'Thanks for picking me up, Charlie,' she said, putting her case in the back and then climbing into the passenger seat.

'You're welcome. Sorry I'm a bit late.'

'It's OK. It gave me time to grab another coffee.' She fastened her seatbelt. 'I assume this is yours, rather than the farm's?'

He'd swapped his BMW for the Range Rover when he'd accepted the job as farm manager, having spent the previous six months suffering the suspension of Mike Newton's ancient pickup truck on the rutted farm tracks. 'Yes, though your parents are both insured on it. Assuming you drive, I can add you to the insurance while you're here.'

'Thanks, but I'll borrow Mum's car,' she said. 'I don't fancy parking something this big.'

'I see you're wearing sensible clothes.' The words blurted out before he could stop them. Thank God he hadn't said something stupid about how the denim suited her curves. Even though it did.

She rolled her eyes. 'It'd be a bit stupid to wear a dry-clean-only dress or high heels on a working farm—and obviously I'll change into wellies when I'm at the farm, because I don't want to have to stick these shoes in the washing machine every day.'

'Sorry. I didn't mean…' He shook his head. 'Sorry.'

'I know. I didn't mean to snap, either. I'm just a bit…' She tailed off.

He glanced quickly at her. 'Anxious about going back to the farm?'

'It's been a while,' she said.

Since before he'd started his project at the farm. At least three years, by his reckoning. 'What happened? Did you fall out with your parents?'

'No. And I don't have a problem with you managing the farm or buying into the business either, before you ask,' she said. 'I know Dad always hoped I'd take over from him, but we all knew it was never going to happen. I'm just not a country girl at heart. I love London. I love the glitz and the glamour and the lights and the noise, and that's where I want to live. I know Dad was disappointed, but we've made our peace with it over the years.'

'But you're still antsy about going back.'

She blew out a breath. 'Yes.'

'Why?'

She grimaced. 'You know why I hate it in West Byfield. It's a small town where everyone's way too interested in everyone else's business. If you don't fit in with everyone's expectations, you're an outsider.'

'Is this about what happened on prom night?' he asked, remembering how she'd cried on his shoulder.

'When I found out that everyone except me

knew that Damien Price had only asked me as his date because he thought I'd be so grateful that I'd give him any sexual favour he asked? No.' She grimaced. 'It started years and years before then. High school was a total nightmare.' She shook her head. 'Sorry. Ignore what I just said. It's a hangover from…a long time ago. I'm over it.'

It didn't sound like it to him.

'Want to talk about it?' He kept his voice gentle.

'No.'

He didn't say anything, and eventually the weight of the silence seemed to grow too much for her. She sighed. 'Infant and junior school were fine. It was high school that…' She broke off and swallowed hard. 'It was nothing physical, no hitting me or stealing my bag or tipping my lunch on the floor—but that old thing about "sticks and stones may break my bones but names will never hurt me" just isn't true. The name-calling makes you feel a little bit less valid, every single time. And every day I had to psych myself up a little bit more, so I could walk in with my head held high and pretend I couldn't hear what they were saying about me.'

He ached for her; at the same time, he admired how she hadn't let the bullies' behaviour crush her spirit completely.

'And oh, dear God, when my periods started…
I was terrified I'd leak or something and it would
give them even more ammunition.' She grimaced. 'The name-calling changed the way I
saw myself. I wasn't Eleanor Newton any more,
the girl whose family had farmed this land for
generations and who used to find the first bluebells every spring and bring some in for the
whole class to enjoy. I was Smelly Ellie Moo-ton,
who smelled of cows or sour milk. Even though
I was pretty sure I didn't smell, it made me para-
noid. I bought the strongest-smelling body spray
I could find, but that was so obvious and it made
the teasing worse. And if they weren't claiming I
smelled, they'd call me "heifer" because I wasn't
stick-thin, like the popular girls.' She blew out
a breath. 'Sometimes I wonder how the hell I
made it out of high school without developing
an eating disorder.'

'I'm sorry you had to go through that,' he
said. 'Kids can be vile.'

'In a pack, definitely. On their own, with no
chance of anybody seeing them talking to me
and then picking on them, too, some of them
weren't so bad.'

'Didn't you tell your parents?' he asked.
'They must've noticed you were miserable.'

'Yes and no,' she said. 'I did tell them, and
they went up to school to have a word with the

teachers—but that just made things worse. It kind of upped the challenge—to get at me in a way where they couldn't be caught doing it.'

'And you didn't want your parents to go to the school again, in case it made it worse still?' he guessed.

'Partly,' she said. 'But also Mum was under a lot of pressure at the time. Grandad died when I was still in junior school, and then Gran got dementia. Mum and Dad didn't want her to go into a home, so Mum looked after her. I could see how worn down my mum was getting, and I didn't want to add to her burden. I guess I wanted to protect her and not let her know how bad things were for me. And Dad was working all hours, so he was too tired to notice much when he got in. I couldn't dump it all on them.'

'I had no idea,' he said.

'Why would you? You were three years above me at school and, although your sister wasn't one of the bullies, she wasn't a friend either. I didn't really have friends at high school.' She shrugged. 'In a way, it did me a favour. I used to go to the library at lunchtime so I could get away from them. I lost myself in books. I discovered really wonderful poetry—and Shakespeare. That made school bearable, and it meant I didn't have to make Mum's life even harder.'

Her smile faded. 'Though, deep down, it didn't stop me wanting to be accepted for myself.'

'You're accepted for yourself now,' he said.

She shook her head. 'In London, yes. In West Byfield, the memories come back. That's why I hate being called Ellie. It rhymes with "smelly". And I'm not that person. I never was.'

'Maybe,' he said carefully, 'you could look at it a different way. It's a pet version of your name, and it's a pretty one. People don't call you Ellie because they're trying to make you feel bad—Eleanor or even Elle sounds a bit formal and distant, so calling you Ellie is their way of showing they want to feel close to you.'

She didn't look convinced.

'But I get where you're coming from, and I'll try to remember to call you Elle, in future,' he said.

'I appreciate that,' she said.

And oh, the bravery in her smile. He knew exactly how that felt. He'd pasted the same expression on his own face every time someone asked him how he was. Lied through his teeth, because how could you tell someone that you felt like a paper husk and the better part of you had been ripped out and buried in your wife's grave?

'I'm trusting you not to say anything to Mum and Dad about what I just told you,' she added.

'I don't want them made to feel guilty about something that wasn't their fault.'

'Of course.' Clearly Ellie—*Elle*—was deeply protective about her parents.

All the same, he couldn't quite drop the subject. 'But you're successful now. A first-class degree, an amazing job. Why didn't you come back to rub it in the bullies' faces?'

'If I was the CEO of a billion-pound company, I'd still be Smelly Ellie or Heifer to them,' she said. 'And I know it's their problem, not mine, but...' She sighed again. 'Actually, it wasn't just people at school. Every boyfriend I brought home from university and beyond dumped me within a week of visiting Bluebell Farm. They couldn't cope with the reality of life in the country—that a dairy farm doesn't mean scones out of the oven every five minutes and roses round the door, it means crazily early mornings and mucking out the byre.'

'It sounds as if you dated the wrong kind of man,' he said.

'I'm very, very good at finding Mr Wrong,' she said. 'Which is why I've given up dating and I'm concentrating on my career.'

Was this Elle's way of making sure he didn't get the wrong idea and think she was interested in him? Charlie pushed aside the thought that he might be interested in her. He'd tried dating once or twice, since Jess's death, but it had never felt right. And it would be way, way too complicated if he got involved with Elle.

'Speaking of which,' she said, 'I wanted to use the travel time to talk to you about the farm's website. I looked at it last night and it's marginally worse than having no website at all.'

'We don't have time to do an all-singing, all-dancing thing,' he said. 'I can't spend an hour a day updating a website.'

'You don't have to,' she said. 'But you do need to organise it better. A website needs to be easy for the customer to find what they want, and easy for you to update. At the moment, the farm's website doesn't work hard enough. You need a calendar and a booking system for the accommodation, at the very least. Not to mention much better pictures and customer testimonials.'

'Flashy booking systems are expensive. People call us if they want to book,' he said.

'You said that yesterday. And is the landline diverted to a mobile when nobody's there to answer it?' she asked, her tone slightly caustic. 'Are you available at, say, nine p.m. when people are browsing their holiday options post-dinner and want to book?'

He sighed. 'It goes to an answering machine, out of office hours. Or they can email us.'

'Meanwhile, the customer gets fed up waiting for an answer and books elsewhere,' she said. 'And you're definitely missing an opportunity with the farm shop and café. You need a sample menu and possibly a booking system, and consider letting people order stock online. I'll have a word with someone about the logistics of online merch—you might need to start off with just mailing the non-perishable goods first.'

'And who's going to deal with that?'

'I'll tell you when I've had a chat to the farm shop and café staff,' she said. 'Because we need their input, too. Obviously I'm not going to give you a hard time about not having any wedding stuff on there, because that's a new thing. We need to think about how you handle it. And, on the education side, you need to list the courses you run. What you've got at the moment is a bit vague.'

'People—'

'—ring you to book. Yeah, yeah.' She shook her head. 'Thirty years ago, that would've been fine. Now, it's nowhere near enough. Again, you need a minimum of photographs and customer testimonials, so people can see what they're getting for their money and hear how much other people enjoyed it.'

'Anything else?' he asked, very slightly nettled by the criticisms, even though he knew she had made some valid points. He couldn't help thinking that, if she'd ignored her past and come back to the farm earlier, she would've seen all this for herself and done something about it. Though at the same time he knew he was being unfair. She'd tried to cope with the bullying and protect her parents from the extra stress when her grandmother was ill—and that was a big ask of a teenager. In her shoes, would his little sister have coped any better? And Elle had done well for herself at work. She hadn't let the bullies of her teenage years wreck her confidence in what she did; though he rather thought they might have trashed her confidence in who she was.

'How often do you update the farm blog?' she asked.

'It's done on a need-to-post basis.' He couldn't remember the last time he'd updated it.

'If you want people to follow it and spread the word about the farm, you need to set up a regular schedule. It doesn't have to be every day. If readers know you post something, say, every Monday and every Friday, they'll come and look at the blog on Mondays and Fridays, expecting to see a new post. If you just post at random times, they're less likely to find something new whenever they click on the blog, and they'll soon stop bothering to come back.'

'Right.'

'Don't get huffy with me,' she warned. 'You're the one who asked me to look at it and make suggestions. I wouldn't be doing my job properly if I patted you on the head and told you what a good boy you are, when actually it's terrible and a twelve-year-old could do a better job.'

'You really don't mince your words, do you?' he asked. 'Would you say all this to your parents?'

'I might be a bit gentler with them,' she conceded. 'But you're the farm manager, and you're the one who's briefing the agency. This is under your remit. Dad, bless him, wouldn't know one end of a computer from another. He rings me to talk him through sorting out his mobile phone when he gets in a muddle. If it was a cow, he'd know everything there was to know about it. But a phone or a computer...' She chuckled. 'Dad's never going to be a silver surfer. I couldn't see any links on the website, but I'm assuming you do have proper social media?'

'There's a Facebook page,' he said.

'Which gets updated how often?'

'Occasionally,' he muttered. When he had the time and the inclination: and no doubt she'd say the same about that as she had about the blog.

'What about Instagram? Twitter?'

'There isn't time. Ellie—*Elle*,' he corrected himself swiftly, 'our focus is on the farm and the conservation side of things, not social media.'

'You can do both,' she said. 'Once it's set up, I can look after it remotely and I can schedule posts in advance for you. I'll tell you what I need and when, and I'll chase you if you don't deliver.'

'You're scary,' he said.

'I'm good at my job. Just as I assume you're good at yours, or Dad wouldn't have appointed you as the farm manager or let you buy into the farm,' she pointed out.

'Thank you. I think,' he said. Though, given the organisational skills and clear-sightedness she'd just demonstrated, he was pretty sure Elle would've made an excellent farm manager. She just hadn't wanted to do it.

'Talk me through the farm,' she said.

'I think it'd be easier to show you when we get there, and then you can ask the questions that occur to you as we go round.'

'Good point.' She made a note. 'We'll do that bit later. So we have the glamping. I'll take a proper look round the shepherd's huts and the farm cottages when we're between visitors, but I want to know about the rest of it.'

'Is this an official briefing meeting?' he asked.

'It's information-gathering for me,' Elle said. 'You know all this stuff, so you're perfectly capable of driving and talking at the same time.

'Got it,' he said.

Charlie had worked in banking, a fast-paced industry where wasted time definitely cost money. Surely he realised it was the same in any industry? Or did he have rose-tinted glasses about farming? she wondered.

She gave him a sideways glance. In Ray-Bans, faded jeans and an equally faded blue T-shirt, he looked a lot more down to earth than he had at the agency in his sharp suit. A lot more approachable. *Touchable.*

And there were a million reasons why she wasn't going to go there.

'The website could work a lot harder for you. It needs to be easy for the customer to use and easy for you to update,' she said. Before she could start fixing it, she needed to work out a brief. To do that, she needed to know more about the farm. And she hadn't missed the irony that she ought to know an awful lot more about her family business, the place where she'd grown up, than she actually did. 'What brings in the biggest income stream?'

'Glamping, followed by the courses,' he said. 'Obviously when the wedding stuff starts, that's potentially a bigger income stream.'

'Got it. Start with the glamping,' she said. 'What exactly does Bluebell Farm offer glampers?'

'Self-catering accommodation for people who

want a proper rural experience and to work on the farm,' he said.

Which she knew meant more than just chilling out in a luxury shepherd's hut. He'd mentioned earlier that some of them helped with the rewilding. 'And what can they actually do on the farm? I know you said you'd show me, but what does the rewilding actually mean?'

'Restoring the bigger natural processes and minimising human intervention,' he said. 'It's everything from repairing fencing through to planting new bits of hedges; and from clearing brambles in the wood so the bluebells have space to grow through to working with the livestock.'

She coughed. 'Are you seriously telling me you're trying to sell shovelling manure out of the barns as a *holiday*? That's going way beyond "where there's muck, there's brass".'

'If you live in the city, you work in an office and you never see the stars at night, then staying somewhere you can actually see the skies and working on the farm is so completely different from your usual life that it's a holiday,' he said.

It was a fair point. Wasn't that why she'd chosen her own career? She'd wanted something glamorous and sharp that was the polar opposite of her lifestyle growing up. Though she still found it hard to believe that anyone would want to muck out the cattle for fun.

'Working on the land—and with the live-stock—reconnects people to nature,' he said.

OK. She got that side of it. Giving people the chance to feel they were making a difference and helping to save the planet. 'I assume you're looking at organic certification?'

'It goes with the territory of rewilding,' he said dryly.

'OK. What else do they get, apart from accommodation and work? Do you feed them?'

'They get breakfast and lunch included at the farm café,' he said, 'and their evenings are their own. We don't do evening meals, but we've negotiated a discount for our holidaymakers at the Red Lion if they don't want to cook for themselves.'

The nearest pub in West Byfield. 'Good.' She made more notes. 'The food at the café: are the ingredients local?'

'As far as possible,' he said. 'Everything in the farm shop's produced locally, from the jams to the chocolates to the ice cream. A local bakery supplies our bread, every day your mum or Lisa who runs the café makes the cakes, and the cheese is mostly our own.'

'Which means lower food miles. Good. That's all stuff I can work with, and the photo opportunities are perfect,' she said. 'What do you sell in the farm shop, apart from food?'

'Local wine, local beer, and local handicrafts. Rosie in the village takes our wool after shearing and spins it. She runs a course here on spinning, for those who are interested.'

'Spinning,' she said, taking a note. That definitely offered photo opportunities. From farm to wear: cute lambs, sheep being shorn, the fleeces, someone spinning the wool, and someone wearing hand-knitted products.

They'd need a few photoshoots; but they might be able to save money on the budget if she could use local people as models. And Charlie Webb would make the perfect model for a high-end hand-knitted sweater. Could she talk him into it?

'What other courses do you run?'

'How to make artisanal dairy products—using milk from the rare breed cattle and sheep—plus photography, art and guided nature walks.'

'What sort of nature?'

'Wildflowers, trees, birds and insects,' he said. 'We tailor it to the group's knowledge.'

'And who runs them?'

'Your dad and I do the nature walks,' he said. 'Your mum runs the dairy stuff, and a local artist runs the art and photography courses.'

Perhaps she could do a deal with the artist for artwork and photography, if Charlie didn't already have what she needed. 'Good.' She thought about what she'd expect to buy from a farm shop. 'Do you sell any toiletries?'

'Yes. They're locally made, too. We include travel-sized ones as part of the welcome basket for the holiday lets.'

'Good.' She made more notes. 'So do you run events at the café? Say, a knitting morning, or crafting-and-coffee sessions, or toddler group?'

'No.'

'That's something to think about,' she said. 'You said earlier about the farm being part of the community. Maybe it's worth looking at what else is offered in West Byfield and when the café's less busy times are, and see if we can fill some gaps.' She paused. 'Would you have time to run me through a nature walk and a typical day in the life of one of the holidaymakers?'

'Are you offering to clean out the byre or milk the cows?'

'I've done my share of that already, over the years,' she said. Then she took a deep breath. 'But it wouldn't hurt to refresh my memory.' Despite the fact she hated the idea of being dragged back to the past.

He pulled into the long driveway that led to the farm.

'We'll continue this later,' she said. 'I need to see Mum and Dad, first, but perhaps you can show me round and we can have a working lunch or something to brainstorm a few ideas.'

'Fine by me,' he said as he parked outside the farmhouse. 'I'll bring your case in.'

She smiled. 'Thanks, but it's not that heavy—and, even if it was, remember I grew up lugging hay bales around.' At his raised eyebrow, she said, 'And I do weights at the gym twice a week. Respectable ones.'

'That's me told,' he said, smiling back and following her into the farm kitchen.

'Ellie! It's so good to have you home,' Angie said, wrapping her daughter in a bear hug. 'I've got the kettle on. I'm running a course at ten, so I can't stay, and your dad's with the rewilding visitors, but—'

'Mum, it's fine,' Elle cut in, returning the hug. 'I'll see you later and we'll have a proper catch up. Charlie's going to take me round the farm, and I'm going to ask him so many questions he'll be bored with the sound of my voice.'

'That's pretty much what I hired you for,' he said dryly.

'Yes. Though, as I said to you in London, I would've done this for nothing, if Mum and Dad had asked,' she said, hammering home the point.

'But you're so busy in London,' Angie said.

Guilt seared her. 'I'm never too busy for you and Dad, Mum, and I'm sorry if I've made you feel that way,' she said, hugging her mum. 'Go and teach your students. And I'll cook dinner tonight.'

'I've already prepped lasagne—a veggie one for you, and an ordinary one for your dad and me. They just need forty minutes in the oven,' Angie said.

Elle's favourite dinner, as a teenager; she blinked away the threatening tears. 'Well, I'll make the garlic bread and put the salad together, as well as heating the lasagne.'

'Charlie, you will eat with us tonight, won't you?' Angie asked. 'There's plenty.'

'Surely you'll want to have Elle to yourself?' Charlie asked.

'There's always a place at our table for you. You're practically family,' Angie said.

Elle noticed the hopeful look in her mum's eyes and sighed inwardly. Please don't say her mum was planning to try to set her up with Charlie. Apart from the fact that her mum had given Elle had the impression that Charlie still wasn't over his wife's death—otherwise he wouldn't still be single—she and Charlie weren't right for each other. They wanted different things.

Guilt flooded through her again. She knew how much her mum wanted grandchildren; she'd seen the wistfulness on her mum's face when Angie had spoken about a friend's new grandchild. This was just another way Elle was letting her parents down. Not taking over the farm, not producing the next generation to hand it on to...

She shook herself. 'I'll make coffee, and then we'll get cracking on the farm tour,' she said. 'See you later, Mum. Love you.'

Once Angie had left and Elle had made the coffee, she turned to Charlie. 'I'm sorry about that. If you'd rather not eat with us tonight, I'll make an excuse for you.'

'It's fine. You and I have a working relationship,' Charlie said. 'We might end up being friends, but that's about it.'

'I'm glad we're agreed.'

'If it helps,' Charlie said, 'my mum's the same. She thinks I...' He stopped.

'Should've done all your grieving by now?' Elle asked.

'Ah. So you know,' he said, bracing himself for the usual pity.

'Mum told me. Not to gossip, but to warn me so I didn't put my foot in it. I made her tell me when she said she wasn't sure if you were really OK with the wedding idea.' She looked at him. 'The way I see it, everyone handles the tough stuff in their own way. You'll move on when you're ready. And, in the meantime, I'm guessing you're sick to the back teeth of everyone thinking of you as "poor Charlie".'

'I am,' he admitted.

'The nearest I've been in your shoes was losing my grandparents, but losing the person you chose as your life partner must be a lot tougher. And that's meant to be sympathy, not pity,' she added.

'Thank you,' Charlie said.

'For business purposes,' Elle said, 'I'm going to ask you the difficult question. Are you really OK about setting up hosting weddings?'

'Yes,' Charlie said. 'For business purposes, I can tell you that I had a happy marriage. I loved Jess and she loved me.' Funny, he could say her name in front of Elle without the usual tight band round his chest. Maybe because Elle had already been so honest with him about her own situation. 'We had a ten-year plan. Work hard, earn a pile of cash—she was a corporate lawyer, so we were both on good money—and then move out of London, find a place in the country and settle down. Kids, horses, dogs, maybe a few other animals. But then she was cycling to work when a guy paying too much attention to his phone clipped her in his car. She came off her bike and hit her head in the wrong place. And she never woke up again.'

'That's tough,' Elle said. Though he was relieved to see sympathy rather than pity in her face.

'We were getting there. We'd even talked about starting our plan a bit early—we were both fed up with working stupid hours and not seeing enough of each other. And then it was too late.'

'Is that why you did your Masters?' Elle asked.

He nodded. 'I still wanted the life we'd planned. And I couldn't bear being in London any more, without her. It felt stifling. I couldn't breathe. And people never stopped talking; it was endless noise, endless traffic, endless mobile phones. I needed wide skies and rolling countryside. Your dad agreed to let me do my final project here because he'd been thinking about changing the farm's focus—just so you know, I haven't pushed him into doing any of the rewilding.'

'I know,' she said. 'Apart from the fact that I checked with my mum, I know that Dad wanted to turn the farm organic years ago and sort out the hedgerows. But it takes time and money.'

'Yeah.' He looked at her. 'Thanks for not wrapping me in cotton wool.'

'No problem. Thanks for not minding that my mum had an unsubtle moment,' she said.

Charlie realised that he actually liked this woman. He'd assumed that by never coming back to Bluebell Farm she'd become a hard-hearted city girl; but that wasn't who she was. Elle Newton was clear-sighted and honest, and he liked that. He liked *her*.

'And obviously,' she said, 'I'll keep what you've told me to myself.'

Just as she'd asked him to keep the stuff about the bullying and her awful boyfriends to himself. 'Thank you,' he said. 'We're officially the keepers of each other's secrets.'

'Good. Now, let's go and look at the farm.'

'I should probably warn you that we had a few April showers last night,' he said.

She looked at her canvas shoes. 'I'd better raid the boot room,' she said, and disappeared from the kitchen. She came back a couple of minutes later wearing green wellies.

'Do you tell the holidaymakers to bring wellies with them?' she asked.

'Yes. I did suggest hiring them, but your mum said that was ick.'

She laughed. 'It's *very* ick. There's a big difference between hiring out bowling shoes you can sanitise easily, and wellies.' She paused. 'Though you could stock them in the farm shop; or, if the shoe shop's still in town, do a deal with them so the holidaymakers get a special offer.'

He loved the way she could make those business connections so easily. Hiring her to do the farm's marketing had definitely been the right decision. 'I'll add it to my list,' he said.

'I'll leave it on the master list, for now,' she said. 'We can divvy things up later.'

Focused, bright and organised. The more Charlie got to know Elle, the more he appreciated her. 'Done. I'll grab my wellies from the car, and we'll start with the cows,' he said.

CHAPTER THREE

WALKING THROUGH THE farm again felt odd. When Elle had last been here, the farm had been half arable and half dairy. There definitely hadn't been a car park; from the looks of the gravelled area filled with cars and the full bike racks at one side, her mum had quite a few students in her class, there were holidaymakers staying, and yet more people were visiting the shop or the café.

Making mental notes, she followed Charlie to the field where the cows were grazing. It was a much, much smaller herd than the one she remembered; a different breed, too. It was familiar, yet at the same time unfamiliar, and Elle found it slightly unsettling.

'These are the British Whites,' he said. 'They're all named after berries.' He introduced her to the two nearest ones. 'This is Elderberry, and this is Juniper.'

Cows.

Smelly Ellie Moo-ton.

But her father had always been really scru-pulous about the hygiene of his cows. Until the teasing had started at high school, Elle had loved their cows, too. She'd thought of them as almost like oversized dogs—she remembered them lowing when they saw her, just as a dog would woof softly and wag its tail in greeting, and they'd loved being petted and scratched be-hind an ear, just like her dad's yellow Labradors.

'They're so pretty.' Their coats were white and they had black noses, black ears and feet; some had a dusting of black spots on their legs. 'Seriously, Charlie, they're really photogenic. Why on earth aren't you using them as poster girls for the farm?' she asked.

'I guess,' he said dryly, 'that'll be your decision.'

'No. It'll be my recommendation, which is a different thing altogether,' she said. 'So they're dairy rather than beef?'

'They were dairy cattle until the middle of the last century. Nowadays, they're seen more as a beef breed, but we're keeping our girls as dairy and to build up the breed,' he said.

'Got it. Hello, you beautiful pair.' She petted them, scratched them behind the ears, and the cows rubbed their faces against her.

'I thought a day in the life of a cow would make a good piece on the website,' she said. 'I'm assuming that the guests like to learn or watch second milking?'

'Yes.'

'Then I'd like to film you milking the cows.' She smiled. 'Do you sing to them?' Her dad had always sung to his cows during milking.

'Ye-es. Though my singing is a long way from being rock star standard.'

He'd definitely look like a rock star, if he was wearing tight jeans and a white shirt. Sexy as hell. The thought made her feel hot all over, and she really needed to get a grip. Charlie could well end up being the face of the farm, and having the hots for him wasn't going to help her do the job properly. 'It doesn't need to be good. We want this to be real. So guests feel comfortable.'

'OK,' he said.

Juniper nudged Charlie with her nose.

He groaned. 'You're worse than a Labrador, Juni. You know I've got cow cake in my pocket, don't you?'

The cow lowed softly and he took a piece of cow cake from his pocket, holding his palm flat so she could take it from him.

Elle couldn't resist filming him on her phone; and she was rewarded big time when Juniper licked his face.

'I had a calf who used to do that, when I was little,' she said.

'Yeah, our girls are all big on kissing,' he said with a grin.

Big on kissing.

An image slid into her head: Charlie Webb, kissing her, his mouth warm and sweet and tempting…

No.

Absolutely not.

'It's good for exfoliation,' she said instead. *Stop thinking about kissing.* 'I'm thinking about how we can save on the budget. Would you be up for being the face of the farm?'

'Me?' He looked surprised.

'Dad might contribute some words, but wouldn't be comfortable working with a photographer— even if I'm the one taking the shots,' she said.

'So you're not saying you think I'm vain?'

It took her a moment to realise that he was teasing her. She smiled. 'Not when you're happy to let a cow kiss you.'

'I used to be vain,' he said. 'In London. Designer suits, silk ties, handmade shoes.'

'You worked in the City.' She shrugged. 'If you didn't dress the part, you'd be marked down, regardless of your ability.'

'I've realised that since being here. I breathe differently,' he said.

She did, too—but not deep and relaxing, the

way he meant. Here, she was on edge and her breathing was shallow.

Not that she wanted to think about that. 'You're beautiful, Juniper,' she said, petting the cow. Then she turned back to Charlie. 'So will you do it?'

He took a deep breath. 'OK.'

'Thank you.' She smiled. 'Obviously I grew up with commercial dairy farming, so my experience is different. Tell me more about a day in the life of a cow.'

'Milking,' he said, 'with a bit of singing. Then it's out to pasture. You might want to film them going through the gate, because they practically kick up their heels with joy at feeling grass under their feet again.'

'Dancing through the fields. I forgot they did that,' Elle said.

'We've got toys for them as well,' he said. 'They like playing with balls.'

'The cows play football?' That would be fantastic. 'I need to film that.'

'They like cow brushes, too.'

'Cow brushes?' It wasn't something she remembered from her years on the farm.

'A rotating bristle brush they can scratch themselves against,' he explained. 'It helps improve their blood circulation and keeps them clean and calm, plus there's less chance of them damaging their skin than if they rub against a tree or a fence.'

'Rotating bristles. So it's something like a car wash brush?'

'Yes.'

She grinned. 'This is all stuff that would be so brilliant for the website. I definitely want to film a football session. That's the sort of thing that's likely to go viral and get you the sort of attention you need.' She looked at him. 'In the interests of transparency, I want the campaign to go viral for two reasons. Most importantly, I want the farm to be a success; but also I'm in line for a promotion. My boss told me that if this campaign does well, the promotion's a definite. Doing well means going viral.'

'Thank you for your honesty,' he said. 'But it's good to know you want the farm to do well, too.'

'So what's next in the life of a cow?'

'The calves go out with their mums. Then it's milking in the afternoon, and we let them stay out overnight when it's warm enough and bring them into the barn when it's not.'

'What happens to the milk?'

'We use it here in your mum's classes, in the café, and for making cheese, butter and yoghurt for the shop.'

She made notes on her phone. 'Perfect. Can we see the calves now?'

'Sure. Actually, they need to come back to their mums, so you can help with that.'

'Bring it on,' she said.

She clearly liked the animals, Charlie thought; at least the bullies hadn't ruined that side of the farm for her. And she looked entranced when he took her to the calves' pen.

'They're beyond cute,' she said, and took a few shots on her phone.

'How old are they?'

'Two weeks. All girls.'

'So they're still feeding from their mums.'

He nodded. 'We put them in here during milking, and let them back in the fields with their mums afterwards. We need to do their bedding, which as you probably remember is shaking straw over the top.'

'Do you still do the knee test?' she asked.

He looked at her in surprise.

'If you kneel on the straw and your knees are still dry, then you know it's thick enough for the calves,' she said. 'Or didn't anyone teach you that?'

For someone who insisted that she belonged in the city, Charlie thought, Elle Newton still had a lot of the country in her. 'No, actually,' he said. 'Thank you for that.'

She made a fuss of the calves as she helped

spread the fresh wheat straw in the pen, and laughed when they sucked her fingers. 'You're gorgeous girls, aren't you?' she crooned to them. 'What are their names?'

'Bilberry, Cranberry and Loganberry,' he said.

'Beautiful,' she said, and snapped some more pics of them.

The reunion with their mums was touching, too, after they'd walked the calves through to the field on a halter and leading rein, and she took more pictures.

The sheep were next.

'Norfolk Horns,' he said, indicating the horned sheep with black faces and legs and white coats.

'I see they've been sheared,' she said. 'And we have a couple of lambs.'

'Those ewes over there are Portia and Helena,' he said, 'and Portia's twins are Viola and Sebastian.'

'One female, one male?' She took a snap of them and looked at him, her eyes glittering with amusement. '*Please* tell me your oldest ewe is called Cleopatra and the ram's Antony.'

'Yes. It was your mum's idea,' he said. Of course Elle would've worked out immediately that they'd named the sheep after Shakespeare characters. She had an English degree. 'Your dad wanted to call them after famous Barbaras, but we got a bit stuck after Barbra Streisand and

Barbara Windsor. That's when your mum suggested Shakespeare.'

'Shakespearean sheep,' she said. 'When I was in sixth form, Mum took me to see this fabulous production of *The Winter's Tale* where they had half the cast dressed as sheep, singing Beyoncé's "Single Ladies".' She grinned, and sang the chorus as 'snippy-snip'. 'There's your new shearing song.'

'Maybe,' he said. He really liked this side of Elle. Relaxed and teasing; clever, yet not arrogant with it. 'We could put Shakespeare quotes on the sheep page, maybe.' He looked at her. 'My A levels were geared to a degree in Economics, so I don't really know much about Shakespeare. Are there quotes about sheep?'

'There are definitely quotes about sheep,' she said. 'I'll dredge them out later.'

When he took her to see the chickens, she gave him a sidelong glance. 'Not fifty of them, then?'

'No. Though their names are shades of grey,' he said, picking up her teasing reference. 'Over there you've got Charcoal, Slate, Pearl, Pewter and Steel. The rooster's called Carbon.'

'They're really pretty, too, with those bright red combs and the silver hackles overlaying the black feathers.' She indicated the feathers round their neck. 'In the sunlight, there's almost a green sheen to the black—like one of those glossy beetles.'

'They're nice hens,' he said. 'They're good-tempered, a bit on the chatty side, and they lay well.'

'Chatty?' she asked.

'They know their names. Rattle a bucket of poultry pellets, and they'll come and tell you they're hungry.'

'Now that's a video for the farm's socials,' she said.

They stood and watched the hens scratching.

'They're free range, then?' she asked.

He nodded. 'They sleep in the hen house at night, but their field's fenced off to keep the foxes out during the day. We use their eggs in the café, in the cakes and the quiches and the breakfasts.'

She took some more notes, as well as photographs.

And she seemed just as entranced by the three hives set next to the wildflower meadow.

'We manage the hedgerows for the wildlife,' he said, 'so there's a high proportion of hawthorn, blackthorn and bramble. The bees like the flowers we have here and seem very settled—and you really should taste the honey.'

Taste.

Definitely a word he should've avoided, because now he was thinking about how Elle Newton might taste: how soft and sweet her lips would be against his. He shook himself. 'I can send you my pictures of the wildflower meadow from last year, but this year's looks a bit sparse while it's at this stage.'

'Last year's pics would be great,' she said. 'And perhaps you can do me some notes on how honey's produced, plus ideas of what's interesting to see and how easy it'd be to photograph. For the honey itself, I can come up with some styling ideas.'

She was definitely in business mode, and her energy and enthusiasm were both infectious.

'I'll do that this evening,' he promised.

She glanced over towards the woodland. 'As it's the end of April, I assume we still have a few bluebells about?'

'Are you thinking about a picture for the website?' he asked.

'Several.' She smiled at him.

Again, her smile made his blood tingle. Charlie knew he was going to have to be careful. He didn't want to risk getting close to someone again and losing them. It had taken him a long while to climb out of the black hole after Jess had died and, even though his head knew it was highly unlikely he'd lose someone else in the same way, he wasn't sure he could persuade his heart to take that risk.

Bluebells, he reminded himself. This was all about the bluebells. The farm. The marketing.

She took a few snaps. 'I'd forgotten just how pretty the woods are at this time of year,' she said.

'The bluebell carpet looked better than this, last week,' he told her.

'This is good enough for my purposes, though if you have photographs I could potentially use that'd be great. And we should encourage visitors to take photographs of the farm and post them—it'll build a bit more on their relationship with us. Maybe the picture of the month could win a goodie basket or something as well as having the photo showcased.' She took some close-up shots as well. 'It's a shame we don't still have a farm dog. One of Dad's Labradors would've looked seriously pretty, sitting among these.' She looked up from where she'd crouched by a clump of bluebells to take a close-up shot. 'I don't suppose you have a friend with a well-trained dog who'd pose for us?'

'No,' he said, 'and I'd be wary about having any dogs around here during lambing.'

'Good point—even if the dogs were well trained, if they're not used to livestock it might be tricky,' she said, standing up.

They walked further into the wood, and her hand accidentally brushed against his. Charlie's skin tingled where it touched hers, and he had to force himself not to grab her hand and cling to her as if he were drowning.

Elle Newton was the first woman he'd really been aware of since he'd lost Jess. For a mad moment, he imagined himself walking hand in hand with her in the wood. What would it be like to kiss her, with the subtle green scent of bluebells in the air, the blue haze of the flowers stretching as far as the eye could see and the birds singing their heads off in the ancient woodlands?

Though he knew things didn't stand a chance of working out between them. They wanted completely opposite things from life; it was crazy to let himself feel like this about someone he knew was so incompatible. He needed to get his common sense back and stop thinking about kissing Elle.

'You know,' she said, 'this would be the perfect place for a proposal.'

'A proposal?' Dear God, he hoped he hadn't mumbled out loud any of those mixed-up thoughts whirling through his head.

'We need a narrative for the wedding side of things,' she said. 'A couple falling in love. A proposal. A party. The wedding itself—or at least a mock-up of one. I assume you're going to show me the barn now?'

'Yes.'

She took his hand and squeezed it gently before releasing it. 'Charlie, are you sure you're really OK with this? It's not stamping on a sore spot? Because I don't want you ending up hurt by the marketing ideas.'

For a moment, his heart was so full of memories and longing and loss that he couldn't speak.

'Charlie?'

He resisted the urge to cradle his hand as if it had been burned. And why did the sound of his name on Elle's lips make his knees feel as if they'd turned to jelly?

'I'm fine,' he fibbed. Yes, it would be like pressing on a bruise; but he wanted the farm to be a success. This was all part of learning to move on. 'Let's go and look at the wedding barn.'

He took her over to the old hay barn, which had been re-roofed and re-floored during the early spring, and new windows let in light all down one side to highlight the gorgeous brickwork and the beams in the ceiling.

'This space is incredible,' she said. 'When I was small, the barn was always full of hay bales. I've never seen it empty like this, before. I had no idea it was this huge.'

'It's big enough to have the wedding ceremony at one end, the wedding breakfast at the other, and then move the chairs from the wedding to the side to give the dance floor,' he said.

'It's perfect,' she said. 'Not just for weddings. You could hire it out for corporate events, too. And maybe for performances—acting troupes, a local Battle of the Bands, that sort of thing. With pop-up food and drink stalls, if we didn't want to use the farm café.'

'Maybe,' he said, pleased that she could see the opportunities in the space.

She walked round it, looking up at the rafters and taking a couple of shots, then at the floor. 'So you opted for wood flooring rather than stone?'

'I talked to your parents about using Norfolk pamments,' he said, referring to the traditional clay tiles of the area, 'but I thought wood would be more practical.'

'Absolutely. It's a smoother surface, so it's less likely that a bride would trip; though, if you had gone for pamments, I would've recommended a carpet for the aisle,' she said. 'I can see this full of fairy lights and woven garlands, and then petals scattered at the sides of the aisle. It'd be magical.'

His own wedding had been very different. He and Jess had got married in Chelsea Old

Church, followed by a reception in the Petyt Hall, with its rich deep red walls and beautiful furniture. Photographs in the gardens, drinks on the terrace. All very London and swish.

Jess would have loved it here, though. Knowing her, she would've spent half her week as a wedding planner and the other half doing *pro bono* legal work, a couple of spaniels curled at her feet when she was at her desk. She would've been a pillar of the local toddler group, then joined the PTA when they moved up to infant school, and...

'Charlie?'

'Sorry. Miles away.' And all the might-have-been had brought back the melancholy. 'What did you say?'

'I asked you to sing me something so I can check out the acoustics.'

Every time he thought he had a handle on who Elle was, she surprised him. Jolted him out of his rut. 'What do you want me to sing?' he asked, feeling slow-witted.

'You sing to the cows when you're milking. Sing me something you'd sing to them.'

'Apart from the fact you're not a cow—'

She laughed. 'Are you quite sure about that?'

He couldn't help laughing back.

What was it about this woman that she could melt the shadows away with a single smile?

'I already warned you, I'm not rock-star standard,' he said.

'You don't have to be. Just enough to give me an idea.' She smiled. 'Or I'll sing and you can do the harmonies, if you like. Dad and I always used to sing Oasis songs when I helped him with the milking.' She started singing 'Wonderwall'.

Elle had a lovely voice, but the words were bittersweet. Had the fire in his heart gone out completely when Jess died? Or was the fire still there, just waiting to be fanned back into life?

She nudged him when she got to the chorus, and he joined in, their voices echoing through the barn.

It felt as if he was actually singing it to her, rather than with her; and it unnerved him slightly. Of course nothing was going to happen between them. This was a job. For both of them. But he couldn't shake the feeling that there was something else there. All he had to do was reach out...

'Yeah, that'll do. The acoustics are great,' she said. 'We can definitely offer this space for performances—music, plays, whatever.' She glanced at her watch. 'I know it's a tiny bit early for lunch, but I had breakfast at a truly ridiculous hour this morning. Have you got time for lunch in the farm café? Or, if you're busy, I'll introduce myself to the team and have a poke about in the shop.'

'I do have some stuff I need to sort out,' he said, knowing that he was being a bit of a coward but wanting to let his common sense straighten his head out again.

'Then I'll let you get on. Actually, I'd like to use the time to have a chat with the team about how things work at the moment, and what ideas they might have for change. And then I'd like to put some initial thoughts together that we can discuss with Mum and Dad over dinner tonight.'

Elle Newton was absolutely driven, he thought. The pace of London suited her.

Yet the farm suited her, too. The way she'd looked when she'd made a fuss of the cows, and that wistful expression on her face in the bluebell woods...

'By the way, I recommend the Brie and chutney toastie,' he said.

'What, a farmer not offering a fry-up or a bacon sandwich?' she asked lightly.

'Afraid not. I'm vegetarian,' he said. 'I have been, ever since I started working here. If someone offered me a steak or a roast beef dinner, now, I'd think of the girls.' He shook his head, grimacing. 'I just couldn't. I'm fine about other people eating meat—it's their choice—but I choose not to, and I'd expect them to respect my choices in the same way I respect theirs.'

'I get that,' she said. 'I'm veggie, too. For the same reason. It made things…interesting, at school.'

'They gave you a hard time for not eating meat?'

She lifted a shoulder. 'It marked me out as different. Though, when one of them tried to force-feed me a ham sandwich, I was sick over him. They never did it again after that.'

'That's disgusting—them, not you,' he said, angry on her behalf. 'I hope you told a teacher.'

'No point. The ringleader smelled of sick all day, and I think it took a while to get the stench out of his shoes. That was enough revenge for me. Yeah, there was a bit more name-calling, oinking followed by vomiting noises, but it's over now,' she said.

'Are you OK?' He reached out and squeezed her shoulder briefly.

'I'm fine. But thank you for being nice about it. I'd better go and chat with the team before the lunchtime rush.'

'Ask for Lisa. She's in charge,' he said as she walked to the door.

Had Elle felt that weird pull of attraction, too, he wondered, and was she using work as an excuse to put some space between them the

same way that he was? Though he didn't want
to think about that and where it might lead. Better to focus on work, too. And he liked the fact
she'd talked about listening to the team's ideas;
it was a good sign that she planned to collabo-
rate rather than impose her ideas on them.

In the cafe, Elle introduced herself to Lisa.

'Ellie Newton. I haven't seen you since I
was a dinner lady and you were knee-high to a
grasshopper,' Lisa said. 'Welcome home.'

'Thank you,' Elle said. 'Though it's a flying
visit. I'm working with Charlie on the marketing for the farm. And if there's any chance you
can join me for a quick chat, coffee and one of
the Brie toasties Charlie just recommended…'

'The Brie's really good,' Lisa said. 'Your
mum makes it. Let's get us both a toastie and a
coffee so you can taste for yourself.'

The Brie and chutney in her toastie—which
were both produced on the farm—were fantastic, as was the coffee. Lisa had cut a small sliver
of the three cakes on offer that day so Elle could
taste them all.

'This is every bit as good as the stuff I buy
from the deli round the corner from my office
in London,' Elle said. 'The presentation's fabulous. I'd love to be able to take shots of all our
dishes, and possibly their ingredients as they're

being made, so we can showcase the fact that we're offering really local food with very few food miles. That's a big selling point on the eco front.' She turned to the next page in her notebook. 'Would it make your life easier or harder if people could book tables on the website? Or is there something else that would be useful?'

By the end of her conversation with Lisa, she'd learned that the café tended to be busy at lunchtime but was quiet between ten and eleven-thirty, and again after four. The room in the barn complex that was used for classes between half-past nine and half-past two would be free for children's parties from four, which would fit in with school times. And between them the café crew had suggested holding stitching or knitting and coffee groups, toddler story time and a silver surfer session, as well as the children's parties based on the activities that the farm offered for younger school classes.

'The library used to run story time and a drop-in silver surfer café, but their opening hours are down to two mornings and one afternoon a week and they just don't have time to run everything, now,' Lisa said. 'There's a playgroup in the village, but it doesn't help new mums with babies and toddlers.'

Elle finished making notes and closed her notebook. 'I'm going to check out what else is on offer at the village hall, and I think you're right: we might be able to fill some gaps in the community,' she said. 'Though when I come up with a potential plan I'm going to run it by you all before I put it in an official report, to make sure you're happy with what I'm suggesting, and I'll have a second look at anything you think needs tweaking.'

'That sounds great. It's good to see you back, Ellie,' Lisa said.

Elle flinched inwardly at the name, but couldn't be mean-spirited enough to correct her to Elle.

'Your mum and dad are so proud of you, but they really miss you.' Lisa gave a rueful smile. 'I know just how they feel. My Mandy's up in Leeds now and, although she video-calls me every week and I read a bedtime story to my grandson, it's not the same as being there by Jack's bedside and getting a hug before he goes to sleep.'

'I'm only back in West Byfield for a little while, Lisa,' Elle warned gently. 'I love Mum and Dad, but London's my home now.'

Lisa gave her a sad nod. 'You never want to stand in your children's way, but sometimes it's so hard. You just want to hold them close again, but you know you can't because you'll have to drive for hours first.'

'Yeah.' Elle had a lump in her throat. Were her parents as sad as Lisa because she'd chosen to live so far away from them? But it was the farm that had driven her away, not them. And, now she was back, her feelings towards the farm were starting to shift again. Charlie had shown her the place in a new light, and she didn't quite know what to think any more.

When she'd finished at the café, she took a look round the shop. As Charlie had told her, they sold produce both from the farm and from local suppliers. The labels were handwritten, but Elle could see opportunities for branding and cross-selling through the website.

There were framed photographs and paintings on the wall, with a discreet price tag to show which ones were for sale. Elle checked her notes and the framed artwork was indeed by Frieda, the artist who ran photography and art classes here, as were the beautiful greetings cards. There were handmade toiletries, ceramics, glassware, and jewellery so pretty that she ended up buying three pairs of earrings, two for herself and one to send to her best friend.

She took a note of the artist's website and phone number, then headed back to the farmhouse. A quick call netted her a meeting later that afternoon with Frieda, and she texted Charlie.

Seeing Frieda this afternoon to brief her on ideas for logo. Let me know if you want to be at the meeting.

And then she settled down to look at what was on offer in West Byfield, and what sort of things their competitors were offering in different parts of the country.

By the time she'd sketched out a list of potential events they could offer and what she wanted to do with the website, it was time to meet Frieda; Charlie had texted back to say that he was sure she knew what she was doing. In some ways, she was pleased that he had so much faith in her; yet part of her was disappointed that he wouldn't be joining her.

Which was ridiculous.

Charlie was her client. Her parents' business partner. That made a line she shouldn't cross.

Frieda turned out to be beautifully receptive to Elle's suggestions and made some excellent ones of her own. Back at the farm, she put dinner on and changed; when her parents came in, she poured them both a glass of wine.

'Welcome home, love.' Mike hugged his daughter fiercely.

'It's good to be back,' Elle said; and, to her surprise, she actually meant it. 'Charlie should be here in a few minutes. And we have a *lot* to talk about.'

CHAPTER FOUR

CHARLIE HAD EATEN dinner with Angie and Mike plenty of times over the last three years. He enjoyed their company.

But tonight was different.

Elle would be there, too.

OK, so she'd said it would be a business meeting, and they'd be talking about her ideas for the farm's marketing plans. But it didn't feel like a business meeting. It felt like a date.

And that in turn made him feel guilty.

This wasn't meant to be about feeling really attracted to someone for the first time in years; it was meant to be about making the rewilding project a success.

All the same, he couldn't stop thinking about Elle, and it felt like a betrayal of Jess.

As he scrubbed himself in the shower, he could almost hear Jess talking to him. *You can't be on your own for ever, Charlie. You need to*

meet someone. You've got so much love to give.
And you need someone to love you back.

Maybe he did. Maybe his family and his
friends were right: it had been five years, now,
and it was time to move on with his life. He'd
done the first part of his ten-year plan early,
moving out of London and buying into a farm
where he had space and animals and could make
a real difference to the area. But maybe he was
using the rewilding project to distract himself
from the fact that he didn't know how to move
forward with the emotional side of his life.

He definitely couldn't face the idea of sign-
ing up for online dating.

Being set up by well-meaning family and
friends had also felt wrong. Even though the
women had been nice, they hadn't been Jess,
and his heart hadn't been in it.

He'd leave it for now. Concentrate on getting
the farm sorted. And hopefully that would keep
his head occupied enough that he wouldn't let
himself get distracted by Elle. By the way her
dark eyes sparkled when she was interested in
something, by the curve of her mouth, by...

'Focus,' he told himself, and turned the temperature of the shower savagely downwards. He
changed into something a little smarter than the
jeans and T-shirt he usually wore, then made
sure he was at the farmhouse at seven on the

dot—not eager and early, yet not trying-too-hard-to-be-casual late.

'Hi.' Elle opened the door and smiled at him.

She'd changed, too. Black trousers, a pretty top, and barely-there make-up. A little more formal than his own work clothes, yet more casual than London office dress; she was good at judging the tone, he thought. He found himself wondering what that soft pink lipstick might taste like, and slammed the brakes on. This evening wasn't meant to have anything to do with kissing Elle Newton.

'My contribution,' he said, handing her a bottle of wine and the locally made chocolates that he'd picked up earlier from the farm shop.

'Thank you. The chocolates will be perfect with coffee,' she said, and stood to the side. 'Come in.'

Why was his heart suddenly beating erratically, just because she'd smiled at him? For pity's sake. He was thirty-one, not fifteen. Getting a grip on himself—just—he followed her into the kitchen.

'We're eating in the dining room tonight,' she said, and ushered him through.

He was used to eating in the farmhouse kitchen with Mike and Angie and whoever happened to be around. This felt way more formal, particularly as she'd set the table with a pristine white tablecloth, silver and crystal.

'Take a seat,' she said. 'I'll bring everything in.'

'Can I help?' he asked.

'Nope. Sit,' she insisted.

He greeted Mike and Angie, accepted a glass of red wine from Mike, and sat down.

She served everything up. 'I'm going to let you eat before we do the business stuff,' she said. 'You can't make decisions on an empty stomach.'

The lasagne—like Elle, he chose the vegetarian option—was wonderful. And he enjoyed the conversation, too. It showed him a different side of Elle, one where she teased her dad about being a dinosaur and swapped recipe suggestions with her mum.

She'd fit perfectly into his family. His mum, dad and sister would love her.

The thought took his breath away. They weren't even dating casually, much less in a place to think about a long-term relationship. He didn't understand where these feelings were coming from: just that they seemed to be bubbling up under the barriers he'd put round his heart, and there didn't seem to be anything he could do to stop them.

'We'll have a break before pudding,' she said.

'This is where you're all going to be working.'
She grinned. 'You won't exactly be singing for
your supper—especially as you're the one who
actually cooked it, Mum, and all I did was heat
it through and put together the salad and the
garlic bread—but I want the three of you sitting opposite me where you can see the screen
of my laptop.'

'This is the first time we've ever seen you do
anything—well, to do with your work,' Mike
said. 'It feels a bit...' He wrinkled his nose.
'Strange.'

'Doing it this way means no wasted paper
with me scribbling things on a display pad, plus
I can't draw a straight line with a ruler,' she said
with a smile. 'Righty. We've got six different
things your customers want to know about. The
first is general information about the farm and
the rewilding. The second is the accommodation and the third is the courses—both of them
need a proper online booking system and calendar, which the office can sort out for me. Then
there's the farm shop, which needs an online
shopping cart; the café, which needs a sample
menu and an online booking system; and finally
the wedding and function room, which is the
one where the customer fills in a very simple
online form with their basic requirements and
you call them back.'

'That's an awful lot of work,' Angie said.

'And I have specialists back in the office who can sort out the forms, the systems and the shopping cart for us,' she said. 'I've talked to Frieda about doing us a logo, so basically people see it and think of us straight away. It'll tie in everything from the labels in the farm shop to the menus in the café, from the wedding brochure to the accommodation brochure, plus the website and the blog and the newsletter.'

She was animated and all lit up, clearly pleased with the work she'd done so far on the project, and her enthusiasm was infectious. Charlie liked the fact she didn't spin everything out. Short, sweet and very much to the point.

'I've been chatting to the team at the café,' Elle said. 'They'd like an online booking system for lunches and maybe for afternoon tea, which I can sort out via the website. And they've got some good ideas about how they can use the quieter times more effectively: if we hold a few more classes before lunch, people will have coffee beforehand and maybe stay for lunch as well. And we could host children's parties after school.'

'How would the parties work?' Charlie asked.

'We'd have one person from the café team in charge, but also make sure there were enough parents attending the party to keep all the children safe. We'd set up in the room we use for classes, so it doesn't matter if it's raining—or we could even use the wedding barn, because that would give them plenty of room. We can run party games in the room, and have a table with a birthday tea at one end,' she said. 'The team suggested we could offer a birthday cake for an extra charge—a hedgehog cake with the "spines" made out of chocolate buttons, perhaps. Lisa's already been looking up templates for a lamb, a tractor and a squirrel. We can also offer goodie bags as an extra—a pencil, a notebook, an animal mask, a packet of seeds, that sort of thing. We were thinking we could do some of the things we already offer on infant school visits: pond dipping, bug hunts, planting a sunflower or something and feeding the chickens or the lambs. And we'd have some indoor games, too: pass the parcel, pin the tail on the lamb—except we'd use magnets on a board rather than something with a pin, so it'd be safer for little ones.'

'I like that idea,' Angie said. 'It's got a lovely community feel about it.'

'That's what the café team thinks, too. I've been looking at what other rare breeds places do. We could consider offering yearly animal adoptions,' Elle said, 'and give the adopter an official Bluebell Farm adoption certificate, a photo of the animal they've adopted, a quarterly newsletter and a voucher for a drink and a piece of cake in our café on their birthday.'

'That sounds doable,' Mike said.

'And we could offer mail order from the shop, or even click-and-collect,' Elle added. 'One of the team at the agency can set up the computer side of it, and we can take advice about the packaging side—perishable foods, ambient groceries and then the non-food items.'

She'd really thought about this, and Charlie was impressed by the fact that she'd got the café team on board before they even considered making changes to the website.

'It sounds as if you've really been busy,' Mike said.

She smiled. 'I haven't finished, yet, Dad. I think it's worthwhile doing a survey to see what people in the area would like us to provide. Lisa said that since the library opens fewer days a week, there aren't as many facilities available for young parents or retired people. We can fill the gap. I've had a look at what other farms in other parts of the country do, and there are some really good courses that mix nature and art— things that I think would work well with what we're doing here. Plant-dyeing yarn would fit in well with the spinning classes and possibly a knitting or stitching club. And there's print making with cyanotypes.'

'Cyanotypes?' Angie asked.

Elle took her phone from her pocket, tapped into the internet and handed it to her mother. 'It's an early form of photo printing, using the power of the sun plus an iron and salt solution. So kids could do it as well as adults. We're looking to attract families as well as couples, right?'

'Right,' Charlie said.

'This is something I would've loved to do as a kid. Or even now. I love the deep blue of the background. The leaves and the flowers look almost like ghosts on the page. I think people will sign up for this in droves, Mum.'

Angie handed the phone to Mike, who peered at it and passed it to Charlie.

'We can use things from the farm to make the pictures—everything from curly ferns through to cow parsley and feathers. The longer you leave the project, the better the detail is. And people on the course can make a print and a couple of cards to take home,' Elle continued. 'Actually, I mentioned it to Frieda, this afternoon, when I briefed her on the farm logo, and she's very happy to run a course.'

'That sounds a great idea,' Charlie said.

'Good.' Elle smiled at him, and again he felt that weird squeezing around the area of his heart. He didn't understand why she was affecting him like this, and it made him antsy.

'Given that we're all about sustainability, I was thinking that we could offer willow weaving classes,' Elle continued. 'There are loads of things we could do. Hearts for Valentine's Day, or to decorate summer solar-powered string lights. Garden trugs, decorations for Christmas, or a willow Christmas tree which can be decorated with ivy and lights for the holidays, and could be used outdoors in the spring and summer to support climbing plants in the garden. Not to mention we could weave the stuff ourselves for the wedding barn: willow hearts for the walls, willow pyramids we can festoon with fairy lights, and a willow arch for the "altar" that we can decorate with flowers. And we can cross-sell everything.'

She ticked off the items on her fingers as she spoke; Charlie could see how she could've persuaded her clients to try something new. Her energy was irresistible, and she was fizzing with ideas: but she was also very aware of the practical side of things and how they'd fit in to the farm's current offerings.

'It all sounds wonderful,' Angie said. She bit her lip. 'But it also sounds like an awful lot of extra work, love.'

'It's not as much work as it sounds, once everything's set up,' Elle said. 'We can keep the newsletter simple and structured: a calendar showing what activities are available for booking this month, and a couple of paragraphs and pictures showing what's happening on the farm this month. You can talk about any new arrivals, or something you've changed or discovered.'

'The thing is, love, we can't afford to employ anyone new to handle this sort of stuff,' Mike warned gently.

'You don't have to employ anyone,' Elle said. 'I can do the newsletter and updates for you in London, in my spare time—not as part of the agency, but as your daughter doing her bit for the family business. You tell me about it, I'll write it up, and then when you've approved the copy and sent me photos, I can put everything up for you on the blog and send the newsletter to your mailing list.'

'I think it sounds a great idea,' Charlie said. 'And I'm happy to liaise with you to do the newsletter and blog.' That would take the burden off Mike and Angie's shoulders.

The brilliant smile she gave him made him feel warm all over.

'I'll do what I can to set everything up while I'm here, for a soft launch,' she said.

'Soft launch?' Mike asked.

'Making a couple of little changes every day, rather than setting it all up and then transferring it over all at once. Word of mouth will get people looking at the farm's website and social media every day. And I'll do the maintenance in London so you don't have to worry about it.'

'I can help with the videos and pictures,' Charlie said.

'Thank you. I think we can start with the things that you're so used to, you take them a bit for granted, but potential visitors would love—things like cows grazing in the field, lambs skipping about, someone bottle-feeding an early lamb where you can see its little tail whizzing round. And people have no idea how loud a sheep sounds when it baas, or that a lamb sounds so much higher-pitched than its mum,' she said.

'Newborn calves would be good, too—when they're still wobbly on their legs and their mum's licking them clean.' Charlie grinned. 'Watching lambs learning to jump is fun, too. That's one of the things that really caught my eye when I was doing my course.'

She made notes. 'And the cows playing football. I am *so* having a video of that on our blog. I've got the caption already.' She raised her eyebrows. 'Moo-ve over, Cristiano Ronaldo.'

Everyone groaned, and she laughed.

'Is it worth filming the chickens?' Charlie asked.

'When they're scratching in the fields? Definitely,' she said. 'And you told me they're chatty. I want to film them chatting to you. Plus we need to borrow some children to play "hunt the egg" and show us what they find. I'll style the eggs for some still shots, too, depending on what colour they are.'

'They're all tinted—that's brown, to you,' he said.

She tipped her head slightly to one side. How cute she looked, he thought. 'Explain tinted.'

'It means the eggs are light brown on the outside, and white inside the shell. It's all because of the pigment protoporphyrin, and when it's deposited on the shell during the laying process,' he explained.

Her dark eyes glittered with interest. 'I had no idea about that sort of thing. It might make a good blog post. Can you give me some facts and figures?'

'Sure. It takes twenty-six hours for an egg to pass through a hen's oviduct, and it takes twenty of those hours for the shell to be produced,' he said, blurting out the first couple of facts that came to mind.

'That's amazing. I had no idea. Can you let me have some more like that, so I can do a "top ten things you didn't know about eggs" post?' she asked.

'Sure,' he said. 'I'll email you later tonight.'

'Great.' She looked pleased. 'I thought we could also cover special days—not just Valentine's Day and Christmas, but things like World Bee Day. We can have videos of the bees in the hive, stills of the wildflower meadow, and maybe put up some ideas of what people can do to help bring bees into their gardens.'

'I've got some notes on bees,' he said. 'I'll dig them out.'

'That'd be brilliant. Thank you, Charlie.'

And again she gave him that heart-squeezing smile, before clearing the table and bringing in a large glass dish which looked as if it contained a rhubarb fool, decorated with little slices of rhubarb. It had the perfect blend of tartness and creaminess, but there was something he couldn't quite work out. Elle had clearly read his expression, because she said, 'I used Greek yoghurt rather than cream, and there's a tiny bit of orange juice and grated orange rind in with the rhubarb.'

'It's lovely,' he said.

She shrugged. 'It's simple and quick. Plus I love rhubarb, so I raided Mum's patch.'

Elle Newton was incredibly capable, he thought. She'd clearly been really busy working on the marketing ideas for the farm, yet she'd produced an excellent pudding as well—food that was good enough to be on the menu of the farm café.

After the pudding, she brought in a platter of cheese and crackers. 'These are all from the farm shop—though I want to actually do one of your cheese-making courses, Mum, so I can take photos and write it up so people realise how awesome it is.'

Though she hadn't just dumped the cheese on a plate and the crackers in a dish; she'd styled it as a proper platter, with tiny bunches of grapes and sticks of celery heart with the fronded leaves still on them, and the crackers were arranged beautifully. Charlie would just bet she'd taken photographs, too, planning to use them to showcase the farm shop's produce. Yet, at the same time, it felt as if she was making a real fuss of her parents and of him, making everything look nice so they'd feel special.

How did she do that, combining her work and her personal life so everything was multi-tasked but didn't feel fake? It made him realise that his own attempts on the farm website really were as hopeless as she'd pronounced them, and he shouldn't have been offended at her bluntness. His own work had been plodding and pedestrian, and Elle would make it sparkle.

'We've pretty much covered everything except the wedding stuff,' she said. 'Until we actually have some weddings whose photos we can use, we'll need a narrative.'

'What sort of narrative?' Charlie asked.

'Show the romantic side of the farm. Watching the sun set over the fields, cuddling new lambs, walking among the bluebells and the wildflower meadow—that sort of thing.'

He knew she was talking about business, but somehow it felt as if those words were purely for him. A personal offer. It was scary and exhilarating all at the same time: as if life was suddenly opening up again in front of him.

They spent the rest of dinner batting ideas around, drinking coffee and eating the chocolates he'd brought, and by the end of the evening Elle's parents had overcome their reluctance to change things and were definitely on board with what she wanted to do to the website.

'Let me do the washing up before I go home,' he said when he helped her take the coffee mugs back into the kitchen.

'No. You have to be up early tomorrow for milking. I'll sort it,' she said firmly.

'My parents brought me up the same way yours brought you up,' he reminded her. 'If I'd cooked, you would've insisted on doing the washing up.'

She spread her hands. 'You've already done your bit. You helped convince Mum and Dad. Besides, the cows won't be happy with me if I make you late for milking. Anyway, I want to talk to you tomorrow about the wedding stuff. Run something by you before I suggest it to Mum and Dad.' She paused. 'Maybe I could do the milking with you tomorrow? At least, I'll bring coffee and talk your ear off, and maybe take a couple of pics for the website.'

Multi-tasking again.

Even though Charlie was enjoying working with Elle, and he liked milking the cows, if he was honest with himself he had to admit they weren't the things he was looking forward to most, tomorrow.

What he really wanted was to spend time with her. For the sparkle she brought to rub off on his life.

'I start milking at half-past six,' he warned.

'I'll be there. The byre, yes?'

'Yes.'

Her dark eyes were huge. For a moment, Charlie wondered if she was going to lean in and kiss his cheek. He realised that he was even swaying slightly forward, inviting her to do it. He'd only had one glass of wine, so he couldn't blame his behaviour on that—or even on a sugar rush from the chocolate. It was all Elle, making him feel a little bit wobbly.

Get a grip, he told himself, and straightened up again. 'See you tomorrow. Thank you for dinner.' His mouth clearly wasn't on track with the programme, because he found himself adding, 'Maybe I can cook dinner for you.'

Noooo. Why had he suggested that? It was practically inviting her on a date.

'And we can brainstorm a bit more of the website,' he added hastily, to make it seem more like work.

'I'd like that.'

Did she have any idea what was going on in his head? Was the same thing going on in hers? He didn't dare meet her eyes properly, and he knew he was being an utter coward. 'Goodnight,' he said, and made a hasty retreat.

Back at his cottage, Charlie looked up the social media links Elle had sent him, using the passwords she'd given him for the accounts she'd set up for the farm. The first picture on *@bluebellfarmnorfolk* was one of the bluebells shimmering in the wood, with a comment about how the farm had got its name. There was a picture of the farmhouse, one of Elderberry eating hay with her head framed in the hay rack, and the three calves, captioned *#moobellfarm*; the chickens, captioned *#notquite50shades #norfolkgrey*; and Portia with Viola and Sebastian, the lambs skipping along beside their mother.

All things he loved; but Elle made him see them with new eyes. The sharpness of the detail. The single bluebell, its narrow bell-shaped flowers bending the stem into a graceful curve, the richness.

Her post was practically a love letter to the farm.

OK, so her job was to sell things—and she'd definitely picked up on the farm's big selling points—but surely it wasn't all surface? Surely she felt a connection to the farm?

Yet he knew why she'd hated it so much here. Ten years ago, he'd had a distraught teenager sobbing on his shoulder after prom about how she didn't fit in with the rest of the school; she'd fled prom when she'd overheard Damien Price saying he'd only asked her to go with him because Smelly Ellie Moo-ton would be so grateful to have a date for prom that she'd definitely have sex with him and... She'd stopped then, clearly not wanting to repeat what Damien had suggested, and instead mumbled that he thought she'd do anything he asked her to. Charlie had a pretty good idea what the guy had suggested.

And then, she'd continued, he'd tell his friends all the details of exactly what she'd done with him, and the whole town would know and despise her. And everyone was laughing at her anyway, because they were all just seeing a heifer in a fancy dress...

Charlie had wanted to find Damien Price, pin him to a wall and make him take on board the fact that you never, *ever* treated a date like that; but he knew that wouldn't help Elle, right then. So instead he'd told her that she was worth far, far more than a selfish loser like Damien. He'd told her to ignore the small minds of the town, and that she could be whoever she wanted to be. The best judge of who she was was *herself* and nobody else.

Clearly she'd taken his words to heart, because she'd gone to university and she'd blossomed; she'd carved out a good career.

And now Elle was back in West Byfield. She'd changed the way she looked, turned herself from scruffy farm girl to elegant city businesswoman; though that was purely surface and Charlie really didn't care about that. The woman he was getting to know was bright, independent and strong, and he really liked her.

He looked further back in her social media feeds. She posted all about the perfect London life: fabulous food, cocktails and stylish coffee bars. There were shots of Elle next to posters for theatre performances and gigs, either on her own or as part of a crowd. He saw what appeared to be a couple of boyfriends in the pictures, even tagged *#Londondate* and *#romance*, but the men seemed to be identikit city types. The type of man he'd been, when he'd been married to Jess, he thought wryly. But none of them had seemed to last for more than a couple of dates. Elle herself had said they dumped her as soon as they saw where she came from.

Even more interestingly, not everything Elle posted was about the glamour of the city. She'd snapped patches of green in London, too, and there were vases of flowers. Perhaps he should've taken her flowers tonight after all, because she clearly loved them.

Maybe she'd join him tomorrow on the nature walk, and he could find out a bit more about what made her tick.

CHAPTER FIVE

IF ANYONE HAD told Elle back in London that a boiler suit and green wellies could look sexy, she would never have believed them. Seeing Charlie Webb in the milking parlour was a revelation. In a boiler suit and wellies, he looked utterly gorgeous.

Or was she just confusing herself and starting to believe the narrative she was creating in her head for the farm?

She'd brought two travel mugs of coffee—remembering from the previous evening that he took his coffee black—and handed one to him.

'Thanks,' he said.

He'd already brought the cows in, and Juniper was tied to the hitching post.

'Can I film some of this for the farm website?' she asked.

'Sure. What do you need me to do?'

'Telling me what you're doing as you're doing it, basically. Introduce me to the cow. Pretend you're talking to people who've never met a cow but might fancy a weekend in the country.'

He looked awkward. 'All right.'

She raised her camera. 'Ready?' At his nod, she started to film.

'Our girls all like us to sing ballads while we milk them. This is Juniper, one of our British White cows, and she likes the kind of songs my parents grew up with.' He broke into 'Hey Jude', changing the name from Jude to Juniper, and Elle grinned, enjoying the wordplay. She filmed a verse and chorus, then stopped the video and put her phone back in her pocket.

He stopped singing and frowned. 'Was my voice that bad?'

She smiled. 'No, but I don't need the entire song. I'll be cutting small clips together to make a single short film. Now talk me through milking.'

She filmed more clips, paying attention to his hands and how he handled the cow. She'd forgotten the scent of warm milk with its faintly grassy tang.

Finally, he finished milking the cow, wiped her teats with dip, made a fuss of her and unhitched her.

'Have you finished filming now?' he asked, looking slightly pained. 'I thought we were going to have the conversation we didn't have last night?'

There was a weird tingling in the ends of Elle's fingers as she looked at Charlie. The conversation they hadn't had. The moment when she'd felt he was leaning slightly towards her, and every nerve in her body had screamed at her to lean right back towards him and touch her mouth to his...

'Uh—yes. The conversation,' she said.

'So what did you want to run by me?' Charlie asked.

'The wedding stuff.' She looked awkward. 'I know this is a big ask, so I didn't want to bring it up in front of Mum and Dad—but you said you'd be the face of the farm.'

'Ye-es.' He'd already agreed that. Why was she repeating herself?

She took a deep breath. 'Could you be our groom, too, until we get a real one?'

'A fake bridegroom?' That was a horrible idea.

His distaste must've shown in his face, because she said hastily, 'Fake's probably the wrong word. What I mean is, would you act as the groom in our narrative?'

His head was spinning. 'I...'

'Don't worry. I thought it was an ask too far,' she said. 'I was hoping we would save on the budget. If you'd do it, we wouldn't have to pay models or agency fees, but maybe I can call in a favour from someone.'

Her expression said it was pretty unlikely. And he'd rather the money for the marketing campaign was spent on something more urgent, like building the booking system and shopping cart. 'What would it involve?'

'We'd be cross-selling everything, showing that the farm's the background to every bit of a romance. The story is that a couple stay on the farm in the accommodation, and watch the sunset together or the sunrise.' She spread her hands. 'Maybe both. A romantic dinner, a stroll in the woods or through the wildflower meadow, an afternoon cuddling newborn lambs. Then a proposal—I was thinking at the beach, to give people an idea of the wonderful bits of the countryside nearby. And we can have the barn all dressed up for a small intimate wedding.'

'And who would be the bride?'

'Me,' she said.

Elle, acting as his girlfriend and then his bride. His heart started to thud. Maybe this would put an extra barrier between them, making her safe to be around. And maybe it was what he needed: pretending to date, as the next step to actually dating. Finally moving on.

It wouldn't be putting his past in a box—he'd always love Jess—but maybe it might be the catalyst he needed. 'Who's going to take the photographs?' he asked.

'Of us? We are. Selfies,' she explained. 'I want to keep an intimate feel.'

Intimate. Now there was a word that made him feel completely flustered.

'So our dinner tonight will be a date,' she said, ruffling his peace of mind even further. 'As far as the website is concerned, I mean. Both of us dressed glamorously.' She narrowed her eyes at him. 'The suit you wore in London will do very nicely.'

'Are you telling me you brought glamorous clothes with you?'

'No,' she said, 'but there are these special things you might have heard of. They're called shops.'

He couldn't remember the last time someone had teased him. And it felt amazingly good. He grinned. 'I'm not sure that West Byfield is up to London fashion standards.'

'I'm not going shopping in West Byfield. Now, is your kitchen tidy, or can we use one of the shepherd's huts?'

His place wasn't untidy, but it wasn't glamorous, either. It was just a place to lay his head.

'Shepherd's hut, I think. Check with your mum.

'Will do.' She smiled at him. 'Right. That's me going on a prop hunt.'

'I've got a nature walk this afternoon, if you wanted to come along,' he said. Because of course she needed to experience it. It had absolutely nothing to do with him wanting her company.

'What time?'

'Half-past three.'

'I'll be there,' she promised. 'It's an hour and a half, right?' At his nod, she said, 'Which gives me enough time to change and cook dinner. Any food dislikes or allergies I need to know about?'

'You already know I'm vegetarian. Nothing else.'

'Good. I'll go and talk to Mum about schedules, and then do my props run.'

'Have fun,' he said. 'See you at half-past three by the café.'

'Perfect,' she said.

And funny how her smile felt as if it lit up the whole world—including the darkest corners of his heart that had been hidden for years.

Elle checked with her mum which shepherd's hut she could use, then borrowed her car and drove into Norwich. She'd made a list on her phone of the clothes that would work in the different scenarios, and it didn't take her long to find what she wanted. She spent a bit more time working on the farm's media plan, including several press releases and the media she wanted to target; and then it was time to meet Charlie and the nature walkers.

He was in the courtyard with six people, whom she assumed were all guests staying in the holiday accommodation. There were two couples of around their own age—she winced inwardly, wondering if that would remind Charlie of himself and Jess—and an older couple who were holding hands. The older couple that Charlie and Jess hadn't had the chance to become.

'Hello, Elle,' Charlie said with a broad smile, and introduced her to their guests. 'Elle grew up here,' he said, 'so although I'm leading the walk I'm pretty sure she'll chip in and correct me from time to time.'

'Think of me as one of the guests. I'm revamping the farm's website,' she explained to the walkers, 'so I'm reviewing what we offer.' She grinned. 'And if you'd like to mark Charlie out of ten at the end, I'm all ears.'

He coughed and gave her a pained look, before saying, 'You really don't have to mark me.'

'I was teasing about that,' she agreed, 'but, seriously, if there's anything you would've liked to see more or less of, please let me know. We want everyone to really enjoy their stay here and get the most out of their time on the farm.'

Clearly she'd said the right thing, this time, because Charlie gave her a warm smile of approval. Except her libido interpreted it rather differently, and her knees felt as if they were buckling.

Somehow she managed to keep herself upright, and she strolled along behind the group as Charlie led them through the meadows, telling them about the cows and the sheep and the chickens, and how they were rewilding the farm. He really knew his stuff; he was able to answer every single question, and he couched it in terms that everyone could understand.

Everyone gave a delighted gasp when they saw the bluebells. 'It's a proper carpet,' one of the younger women said.

'We're getting near the end of the season now, but they've been here a very long time,' Elle said. 'Having this many bluebells in one place is a sign of ancient woodland—it shows that the wood dates back at least four hundred years. I remember coming here with my mum and my gran when I was a toddler, and it was like a sea of flowers.'

Charlie made the group stop and listen in the middle of the woods, and taught them how to distinguish between several different birdcalls.

Elle had never been any good at distinguishing them, but Charlie's words helped her to isolate some of the calls and hear them clearly. He obviously loved this part of country life and looked delighted to share it with others and help them feel the magic, too.

'What's the one that sounds like a rattle?' one of the others asked.

'That,' Charlie said, 'is a magpie who's a bit annoyed about something and making his displeasure known.' He rolled his eyes. 'There's one nesting in the tree outside my bedroom window who likes to wake me at four in the morning using that exact call.'

'It'd drive me *mad*,' one of the younger men said.

'It gets me up in time for milking,' Charlie said. 'But, yes, I admit, if it's not my turn for milking, I can't help wishing it nested on the other side of the wood, so I could get a couple more hours of sleep!'

When they reached the wildflower meadow, Elle couldn't resist asking everyone to name as many of the flowers as they could before she filled in the gaps.

'You know so much about the flowers. Are you a plant specialist?' the older man asked.

'Most of it is stuff my gran taught me when I was very small,' Elle said. 'I used to love walkng by the hedgerows with her and seeing all he different flowers.' She'd forgotten how much she loved it; today had scrubbed away some of the stains of the bullying and let her see the arm for what it really was rather than the place hat had haunted her.

After Charlie had introduced the walkers to he cattle and let them pet the cows, and they'd answered all the questions, they took their guests back to the café.

'I thought we made a good team on the walk,' he said, when the guests had gone. 'Me on the birdsong and you on the flowers.'

'It worked well,' she agreed. 'And I think our guests had a good time and learned a lot. Is that usually how it goes?'

'I try to tailor the talks to whatever they're interested in,' he said. 'But you had them in the palm of your hand with all the flower stuff. You taught me a lot, too—I had no idea about some of the things you were telling them. Soapwort actually being used as soap, and called Bouncing Bet because it looks like a laundrymaid at work.'

'I admit I learned that when I was working in a detergent campaign, but I've always liked flowers,' she said. 'Actually, my guilty pleasure is to go to the flower market at Columbia Road every week and treat myself to a bunch of something gorgeous.' She shrugged. 'Which I guess is better for me than chocolate.' She glanced at her watch. 'See you at six-thirty in Hut Two. Which needs a proper name,' she said. 'We'll brainstorm it.'

'It's a date,' he said. And then his eyes widened. 'Not a *date* date,' he said, sounding awkward.

'Of course not. It's an acting date,' she said. 'For the farm.'

'For the farm.'

And it stung a bit that he sounded so grateful. What would be so bad about actually dating her for herself? Or maybe she was overreacting, because West Byfield still made her feel antsy. Charlie had helped remind her of the times when she'd been happy here, milking with her dad and looking at the wildflowers with her mum and her gran; but the misery of her high school years still echoed in her head. 'See you later,' she said coolly.

What had just happened? Charlie wondered. Elle had been perfectly friendly during the nature walk; she was a natural, responding to the walkers and judging the right amount of detail to keep them interested. They'd agreed to meet this evening, as planned, to start the marketing campaign. He couldn't think what on earth he'd said to upset her. Unless, maybe, she'd realised that he was protesting a bit too much about to-night not being a date. That she'd guessed he was attracted to her, and she didn't feel the same way about him.

He raked a hand through his hair. Or maybe he was overcomplicating things and she hadn't been cool towards him at all; maybe it was simply that he felt guilty for being attracted to her. Survivor guilt, perhaps. He knew Jess wouldn't have wanted him to mourn her for ever, but it just seemed so unfair that she'd never had the chance to live their dreams.

He didn't have any answers, but at least he could distract himself by going to check the fences around the livestock. And he'd need to be back at his cottage in time to scrub up prop-erly for his 'date' with Elle.

Elle walked back to the farmhouse via the blue-bell woods, so she could gather a small posy for the table. Once she'd showered and changed and put together a box of the ingredients she needed, she headed for Hut Two.

She sorted out the main dish first, and popped it into the oven, before setting up the hut for filming. A bit of raffia tied round the neck of a jam jar made it look rustic and chic, once the bluebells were in water. She set the table outside with a plain tablecloth and a candle as well as the bluebells, then went back into the shepherd's hut and prepped the starter and the pudding.

As the minutes ticked by, anticipation started to fizz in her veins. Even though she knew this was just for the farm's website, and they'd agreed it was an acting date rather than a proper date, it *felt* as if she were cooking for her new man. And she hadn't felt like this about a real date in years; she'd dated so many Mr Wrongs that she'd just given up trying to find the right one.

'It's not real. Charlie's your fake boyfriend,' she reminded herself. 'Fake fiancé-to-be.'

But maybe feeling as if it was real would make the photos more convincing. And they needed their potential brides and grooms to see the romance, didn't they?

At precisely half-past six, Charlie arrived. He sniffed the air. 'Something smells fabulous.'

'It's very easy,' she said. 'My go-to dinner party menu in London. You can ignore it and leave it to look after itself in the oven.'

'And you look gorgeous,' he said.

'Thank you.' She inclined her head. 'As do you. Can you open this for me?' She retrieved the Prosecco from the fridge. 'Then we can take a selfie at the table.'

He opened the bottle without spilling a drop,

and poured two glasses. Elle took various selfies of them holding their glasses together in a toast, then put on a playlist of romantic songs. 'Give me five minutes to mess about in the kitchen,' she said.

And she was glad of the break; Charlie, all scrubbed up and in formal clothes, was breathtaking. She'd wanted the romance to look realistic, yes; but she also needed to flatten some of those little flutters of attraction, because it would be too easy to make a fool of herself.

'That looks sublime,' Charlie said, when Elle brought out two plates of griddled asparagus in melted butter, with half a lemon tied in muslin on the side.

'Very, very early English asparagus that I begged off Lisa,' she said, and took photographs of the plate.

It tasted as good as it looked.

Then she brought out a baked mushroom risotto with chickpeas, teamed with a dish of very garlicky wilted spinach and another of tomatoes roasted on the vine. It was a domestic side of Elle he hadn't expected; from what he remembered, London was all about eating out or takeaways, and there was never enough time to cook properly. Though she had mentioned dinner parties; and he already knew she'd inherited her mother's amazing organisational skills. So maybe she really was the sharp city girl she'd told him she was.

She took more photographs. 'This is going to look great as a collage,' she told him. 'The shepherd's hut lit with fairy lights inside—they were an excellent idea, by the way.'

He smiled in acknowledgement of the compliment.

'The table with the candle and bluebells, framed by the lavender,' she continued, 'the food, and us with glasses of fizz.'

'The perfect romantic evening,' he said.

But the weird thing was, even though he knew this was all for show, it *felt* romantic. Like a proper date.

Elle was still virtually a stranger, and yet on a deeper level Charlie felt that he knew her.

'So what's your five-year plan?' he asked, refilling their glasses.

'Promotion to Senior Account Manager, then head of creative, and then maybe start my own agency,' she said.

'So you wouldn't come back here if your parents want to retire?'

'There's no need. They have a perfectly adequate farm manager,' she said.

'I wasn't fishing for compliments.'

'I know.' She sighed. 'But I don't want Mum

and Dad getting their hopes up. I'm not going to come back here with Mr Right and produce the next generation to hand the farm to.'

'You don't want children?'

'It's more that I don't think I'll ever find the Mr Right to have children with. And I'm concentrating on my career,' she said. 'It's not as bad at Bluebell Farm as I remember it being during my teens, I admit. And thank you for reminding me of the bits I'd forgotten I loved about the farm. But nowadays I belong in London.' She paused. 'So what's your five-year plan?'

'The rewilding project,' he said. 'I want to increase the diversity of the flora and fauna. Reverse the decline in numbers of the species we do have.' Which meant living here, not London.

'What about when you've done that?' she asked.

'Consolidation.'

'It's about as far as you can possibly get from the life you had in London,' she mused.

She was right on the nail. 'I needed a change.'

'Would Jess have liked it here?' she asked quietly.

He liked the fact that she didn't shy away from saying his late wife's name. 'Yes. She would've loved the sunrises, being up with the birds in the morning, listening to the skylarks and trying to spot them.'

'Is that what you like, too?' she asked.

'As I said earlier, I can breathe here. I couldn't, in London. Not any more.' He swallowed. 'Not without Jess.'

'It's still hard to cope?' she asked gently.

She was being kind, not prying or smothering him with unwanted pity. 'It's been five years. It's not as raw, not like the early days when I couldn't even get out of bed and I was curled into a ball, sobbing my eyes out.' He looked at her. 'But there are still days where it feels as if the centre's been sucked out of the world. Where I just want to be on my own: me and the fields and the animals and the wide skies. I'll never be able to repay your parents for giving me the space I needed, when I needed it.'

'My parents are great,' she said. 'Which is why I don't want them to know about how bad it was at school, or what really happened at the prom. It wasn't their fault; plus they already had more than enough to handle, with Gran's illness, so I don't want them hurt by finding out about it now and realising I kept it from them.'

That sense of loyalty alone would've drawn him to Elle. Charlie didn't let himself dwell too deeply on what else drew him to her.

'I'm fortunate never to have experienced a

loss like yours—I was too small to remember much about Grandad, and when Gran died I was sad but relieved that she wasn't in pain and just *lost*, any more. My mum's parents were older, when they died, and they'd had time to have a good and happy life together,' she said. 'But I can imagine how hard it must be for you, with Jess being so young and all the things you didn't have time to do together.' She reached out and squeezed his hand briefly. 'You were really kind to me, all those years ago. You made everything bearable, that night. So if you ever need a friend, someone who'll listen and not judge, and keep everything you say completely private, I'm here for you.'

She meant it. He could see the sincerity in her expression. 'Thank you.' But if he opened up to her, if he let her close, if he let himself start to feel again...that was a risk he wasn't quite ready to take. 'I was looking through the stuff you've done for the farm on social media,' he said. 'It's amazing.'

'It's a start,' she said. 'I've asked Frieda to use bluebells in the farm logo; I'm hoping she'll come up with a really simple line-drawing that we can use on the labels of everything we produce as well as on the website. Make it recognisable as ours, and tie everything together.'

'Sounds good,' he said. 'I looked at your social media, too. It looks like you have the perfect life in London.'

'The West End, cocktails, afternoon tea. It's pretty much what people expect to see in my life,' she said with a shrug.

'So it's not real?'

'It is and it isn't,' she said. 'I work hard, but I play hard as well. My socials don't show the admin or the chores, because nobody's interested in that.'

'Aren't they?'

'No,' she said. 'People who come to the Bluebell Farm account won't want to see you wrestling with the accounts, or filing receipts, or ordering cow cake, or even mucking out the byre. They'll want to see the highlights—the bluebells, the newborn lambs and the cows playing football. The stuff that makes them feel all warm and fuzzy.'

'I guess,' he said.

'And, for the record, I love my life in London. Summer evenings with cocktails on a rooftop terrace as you watch the sun set over the Thames, spring when the rain makes Covent Garden glisten and all the wisteria comes out in Chelsea, winter with all the Christmas lights and the sparkly stuff, and autumn when you go to see the deer on a misty morning in Richmond

Park and walk under falling leaves on the Embankment.'

Things that sounded delightful; things that Charlie hadn't done with Jess, because he'd been too focused on work and not focused enough on life outside—just as Jess had been. It had taken losing her to make him get a better work-life balance. Or maybe he'd just swapped one workaholic lifestyle for a slightly different but equally intense one. The pictures Elle had just painted in his head made him wonder if he'd see London differently now.

'You're really happy there,' he said.

'I am,' she confirmed.

'Then we'd better make sure this campaign goes viral, so the farm's a success and you get your dream job,' he said. 'That way, we both win.'

'We both win,' she said, and clinked her glass against his.

Maybe the bubbles had gone to his head, because he held his hand out to her. 'Dance with me?'

Her eyes went wide and her lips parted slightly. Her breathing looked as shallow as his suddenly felt.

'I...' Then she seemed to pull herself together. 'Method acting? You're absolutely right. The best way to write copy about dancing under the stars is to do it first,' she said.

Her words brought his common sense back—but only for as long as it took to stand up and take her into his arms. Then all the sparkly stuff seemed to start up again. Even though the stars weren't out and it wasn't really that dark.

They didn't talk, just danced cheek to cheek. He hadn't danced with anyone since Jess. Yet, although in some ways this should've felt like a betrayal, it felt *right*.

A slow, smoochy dance. Where Elle was close enough that he could smell the vanilla scent of her perfume, a sweetness that undercut her sharp city girl persona. Where her arms were wrapped tightly around his. Where it felt as if his heart was beating time with hers.

His cheek was right next to hers, and her skin felt so soft.

All he had to do was move his head slightly, and the corner of her mouth would be right next to his. And if she turned hers, too, then the angles would be perfect and his mouth would meet hers, and...

A shrill crowing noise split the air, and he pulled back.

Saved by the rooster.

'I thought roosters only crowed in the morning?' Elle said, looking dazed.

Had she, too, thought about them kissing? He pulled himself together with an effort. He needed to get them back on a friend-zone footing. Like *now*. 'According to Carbon, any time of day's good for crowing. It's an "all clear" to let the hens know it's safe to forage.' Plus the rooster had just stopped Charlie making what could've been the worst mistake ever. 'And he's a pretty good dancer, too.'

'He dances?'

'Flutters his feathers, struts his stuff and circles the hen until she says yes.'

She grinned. 'I've seen Carlos Acosta dance "Little Red Rooster" on stage when I was in the front row, so I completely get that. Total stage presence.'

'Carbon has that. Stag presence, perhaps,' he added, hoping that the terrible pun would lighten things up again. He didn't want to think about strutting his own stuff.

She laughed. 'I'm going to make a note of that. And I want a vi—'

'—deo for the farm website,' he finished. 'Got it.'

Carbon was still crowing.

'Not quite the romantic birdsong I would've liked to film,' she said.

'There's always the nightingales,' he said, before he could stop himself.

That made her look at him. 'We have night-ingales?'

'They arrived a couple of weeks ago.'

'Can you show me where to find them so I can film them singing?'

'They do actually sing in the day as well as the night, you know,' he said.

'A nightingale,' she pointed out, 'ought to be filmed at night, to live up to its name. And, actually, it'll be wonderful just to have the sounds of the woodland and a dark screen. Something different. Something to make people use a different sense instead of just glancing at it and scrolling on. Something to make people listen and feel.'

'It's probably a stupid question,' he said, 'but I assume that means you want to do the night-ingales tonight?'

'Given that I'm back in London in less than a fortnight? Absolutely.'

'You probably already know this,' he said, 'but only unpaired males sing at night. They use their song to attract a mate. Hang on.' He grabbed his phone, searched the internet and found her some audio. 'This is what we'll be listening for.'

'That's lovely, all the whistles and trills and gurgles—and it's really loud,' she said, sound-ing surprised.

'They're show offs,' he said with a grin.

'Figures that they're male,' she said dryly.

He raised an eyebrow. 'You really have been mixing with Mr Wrong.'

'That wasn't meant to sound bitter. I wouldn't give any of them the power to take the joy away from my life. Plus,' she added, 'someone very wise once told me that the best judge of who I was was me.'

She remembered what he'd said to her, all those years ago? 'I'm glad it helped,' he said, meaning it.

'If it hadn't been for you, that night, making me see that Damien was the problem, not me, I would've gone right back into my shell,' she said. 'But you gave me the confidence to be myself.' She lifted one shoulder in a half-shrug. 'Right now, I'm in a place where I'm content with my life and I'm happy to focus on work. And I think maybe I've tried too hard to look for Mr Right, so I convinced myself that all the Mr Wrongs weren't really as awful as they turned out to be. So I've stopped looking. As far as I'm concerned, it's time for Mr Right to try and find me.'

'Sounds like a plan,' he said. He wasn't Mr Right for her, was he? Not when they both wanted such different things. Besides, he wasn't looking for another partner. He glanced at his watch. 'We could get changed into something more suitable for woodland, then meet at my cottage at ten.'

'You're on,' she said.

'Actually, I've got a better idea. I'll do the washing up, and bring all your stuff back to you at ten. Then we'll go looking for the nightingale,' he said.

'Are you sure?'

'Definitely.' Because washing up with her would be tricky. The shepherd's hut would make it too intimate: and he'd be very aware that there was a wide bed with soft pillows and fairy lights, only a short distance away...

'Thank you.'

'Take the rest of the bubbles back to your mum and dad,' he said.

'Will do. In the meantime, I'm going to sort out a piece for the website,' she said.

That had been close, Elle thought.

Too close.

She'd almost kissed Charlie. And there was a huge difference between method acting and actually kissing someone for real.

Charlie Webb and his amazing bluebell-coloured eyes could all too easily turn her head, if she let him.

She was still thinking about that kiss as she

handed over the Prosecco to her parents. And as she changed out of her little black dress and high heels into jeans and walking boots. And while she was reviewing the snaps she'd taken on her phone.

The shepherd's hut looked idyllic. The food looked fabulous. And she and Charlie looked as if they were a real couple, laughing into the camera.

'Client. Dad's business partner. Still getting over his grief. Wants the complete opposite of what you want in life,' she told herself out loud.

Why didn't any of the barriers feel enough, even when they were layered together? Why was her mouth still tingling at the thought of his lips brushing hers? They'd been dancing cheek to cheek. He'd held her close, and she'd felt his arms tightening round her.

If the rooster hadn't crowed at that exact moment, she was pretty sure they would've ended up kissing.

And who knew where that might have led?

She forced herself to concentrate on the website. But then she went downstairs to get a drink of water, and realised that it was raining.

She sent a text to Charlie.

Assume weather means nightingale off? E

He replied relatively quickly.

If it's stopped raining in half an hour, still on. Wellies rather than walking boots. C

The weather was clearly on her side, because it stopped raining. Just before ten, she pulled on wellington boots and a light raincoat, and then she heard the knock on the kitchen door.

'Perfect timing,' she said when he opened the door.

For a mad moment, she thought he was going to lean forward and kiss her on the cheek. And a very rash part of her would've been tempted to angle her face so his lips touched hers instead of her cheek.

'Thanks for bringing my stuff back,' she said, and put the box on the kitchen countertop.

He handed her a torch and switched on his own. She followed him to the woods, making sure that she stepped where he did—except for the moment when she found herself daydreaming, and then was aware that she was slipping.

'No!' she yelled, dropping her torch and flailing her arms in the air, trying to keep her balance on a surface that slid away from her.

Charlie's reflexes were lightning-quick; he turned round, saw that she was struggling with the edge of the ditch and was about to fall flat into the mud, grabbed her with the hand that wasn't holding the torch and swung her up to safety.

In one way, it was a good thing, because it meant she didn't make a fool of herself or get covered in mud.

In another way, it was very far from being a good thing, because now they were up close and personal again, and the way her torch had fallen meant that its light was shining straight onto them both. Her breathing was all shaky because of his nearness. Because of his clean masculine scent. Because he was looking into her eyes, and his pupils were absolutely huge.

Pupils dilate to let the light in, her common sense said.

They also dilate when your brain gets a good boost of dopamine and oxytocin, her libido pointed out.

Nah, he was just worried that you were going to fall, her common sense countered.

Yeah, but the hormonal stuff only happens when you're really attracted to someone, her libido said, doing the equivalent of breathing on its nails and polishing them. *He likes you. He really, really likes you. And you like him. You wanted to kiss him, earlier. And it looks as if he wants to kiss you...*

His lips were parted.

So were hers.

And he was close, so close. Not invading her space and marking his physical superiority, but as if he couldn't bear to pull himself away from her.

He was definitely looking at her mouth, as if he was wondering what it would feel like against his. She was looking at his mouth, too. And she saw the very moment he moistened his lips. Her own lips were tingling, too. She'd never wanted to kiss anyone so much in her entire life.

This was crazy. She knew that. All the same, she found herself leaning forward. He leaned forward, too. And then his mouth grazed against hers. Once, twice: almost shy, but oh, so sweet. And she was lost; she slid her arms underneath his, drawing him closer. He cupped her cheek with one hand and lowered his mouth to hers again, soft and tender.

All of a sudden, her skin felt too tight. And she was definitely wearing too much. And she didn't care that it was dark and they were in the middle of the woods: all she could focus on was Charlie and the way his mouth moved against hers, teasing and tempting and making her want more.

An owl hooted a warning, long and low, and he pulled back.

Another avian intervention. Did the entire local bird population want to warn them off each other, or something?

'Sorry. I...' His words trailed off.

She shook her head. She wasn't sorry, and she didn't want him to regret it, either. 'Not your fault,' she said. 'It's the adrenaline from nearly falling flat on my face and you rescuing me. It didn't mean anything.'

'No, of course.'

Elle was lying through her teeth, and she was pretty sure that Charlie was lying through his teeth, too.

That kiss had *meant* something.

But she needed time and space to process it and work out what it had actually meant.

He gave her his torch, then got down into the ditch to rescue hers; he wiped the mud off on his jeans. 'Let's go find that nightingale,' he said.

She walked behind him, hating the sudden awkwardness that had sprung up between them.

Then she heard it.

A sweet, complex song, with short verses and pauses and rippling phrases.

'Is that the nightingale?' she asked.

'No. It's a robin,' he said.

'I want to film this anyway,' she said. 'It's lovely. And so loud.'

'Robins *are* loud,' he said, but he stood still

so she could film the song without the sound of his footsteps trampling through it.

'Done,' she said, when she'd tapped the screen to stop recording.

They walked a bit further, and he stopped.

'Listen,' he whispered.

She couldn't hear it at first, but then she did: a bubbling exuberance, whistling phrases and warbling, even louder than the robin. She recorded a minute of the song, then just listened, transfixed, until the song faded. It was an incredibly beautiful moment, one she wouldn't have wanted to share with anyone else. And it would be very foolish to wish that Charlie was standing behind her, with his arms wrapped round her and his cheek pressed against hers, as they listened to the nightingale singing. It wasn't going to happen.

'"And as it gets dark loud nightingales/ In bushes/ Pipe, as they can when April wears,/ As if all Time were theirs,"' she whispered.

'That's lovely,' he said. 'Poetry, I'm guessing, though I don't know it.'

'It's Thomas Hardy. *Proud Songsters*,' she said. 'It's not the most famous nightingale poem—that'd be Keats or Milton—but it's one of my favourites.'

'I'll look it up,' he said. 'Unless you know the whole thing by heart.'

She wasn't going to stand here quoting her favourite poems. Because it was a short skip from Hardy to Shakespeare and Donne; and she could just imagine Charlie reading her favourite Donne poem to her, his voice low and sensual, undressing her with the poet's words and making her very hot and bothered indeed...

'Look it up,' she said. And her voice *would* have to croak, she thought crossly. She didn't want him thinking that that kiss had thrown her. Particularly because it had. She couldn't remember the last time she'd felt this flustered.

The nightingale started up again, to her relief, and they listened for a while longer. And she made very, very sure she didn't sway towards Charlie, much as she was tempted.

'You've got milking tomorrow,' she said when the nightingale stopped singing. 'I'd better let you get back.'

'I'll see you back to the farmhouse,' he said.

Given that it was dark and she'd already nearly fallen flat on her face, she wasn't going to protest that she could find her way perfectly well by herself. 'Thank you,' she said.

Charlie didn't trust himself to speak on the way back out of the woods. That kiss had shaken him, and he didn't want to say anything stupid.

'If we're quiet on the way back, we might catch more nightingales or robins singing.'

'Good idea,' she said, to his relief.

Though silence didn't actually help. It gave him room to think. To brood about the way he'd kissed Eleanor Newton—and the way she'd kissed him back. The way his skin had felt as if little currents of electricity were running across it. The sweetness of her mouth, her initially shy response, and then the way she'd held him, drawn him close.

He hadn't kissed anyone like that for a long, long time.

What the hell had possessed him?

Elle was the first woman he'd really kissed since Jess. Not that he was beating himself up for being unfaithful; Jess had been gone for five years now, and if he was honest with himself he was lonely. Bone-deep lonely. And he'd chosen this job in part because he could work hard enough to be so physically tired at the end of the day that he didn't have the energy to think.

Jess wouldn't have wanted him to be on his own—just as he would've wanted her to find someone else to love and cherish her, if he'd been the one who'd died. But, at the same time, the idea terrified him: what if he let Elle close?

He knew she didn't want to stay here in Norfolk, and he didn't want to go back to his old life in London. There wasn't any workable compromise, here. One of them would have to give up their life to accommodate the other, and that just wasn't fair—on either of them.

By the time they got back to the farmhouse, he felt prickly and out of sorts. So his tone was a bit gruffer than it should've been when he muttered, 'Good night, Elle.'

'Good night. And thank you for taking me to the nightingales,' she said politely.

She sounded cool and confident and perfectly normal. That kiss clearly hadn't scrambled her brains, the way it had scrambled his. He was the problem here, not her. He shoved his hands in his pockets and hunched his shoulders. 'You're welcome.' And please don't let her ask him in for a coffee or whatever. He didn't think he could face her in a really bright light, particularly as he thought she might be rather good at reading people and seeing what they'd rather keep hidden. 'I'd better go,' he said. 'Milking.'

'Of course.'

He waited until she'd closed the door behind her—he wasn't *that* rude—and then headed back to his own cottage.

A shower didn't help, because he found himself daydreaming about taking a shower with her.

A mug of coffee didn't help, because he thought about having coffee with Elle.

He didn't have a dog to talk to, either. One day he would, but right now he didn't have time to train a pup and it wasn't fair to bring a rescue dog who might not be used to livestock onto the farm.

He didn't have anything.

Thoroughly out of sorts, he went to bed. Though he spent a good half-hour tossing and turning and bashing his pillow, and trying to stop thinking about Elle. And, when sleep finally claimed him, he dreamed of kissing her all over again…

CHAPTER SIX

FACT: ELLE HAD liked Charlie kissing her.

Fact: she'd liked kissing him back, too.

Fact: in a little over a week's time, they'd be a hundred or so miles apart, for the rest of their lives. So it would be utterly, *utterly* stupid to let herself dream about him. Wouldn't it?

It didn't help that she spent Thursday morning helping her mum prepare one of the shepherd's huts for new guests. She kept thinking of the meal she'd shared with Charlie in the hut next door, their slow dance and near-kiss, and then the actual kiss in the woods—a real bone-melting kiss.

For pity's sake. What was wrong with her? She was meant to be focusing on her job and getting that promotion, not dreaming about yet another Mr Wrong. The only way that she and Charlie were going to be together would be on the pictures for the farm website.

'Love?'

Elle's face heated as she realised her mum was talking to her. 'Sorry. Miles away. What did you say?'

'I was asking what you thought of the huts.'

'They're lovely,' Elle said, meaning it. 'Though I think they need names.' She and Charlie had been supposed to brainstorm some names yesterday, but dancing with him had swept it completely out of her head. 'Maybe after flowers? Say, one of them could be Primrose, and all the colour accents could be primrose?'

'That's a great idea,' Angie said. 'I'll have to get wooden plaques made with the names painted on them.'

'The gardens round the huts look nice, too. All the lavender—it'll smell gorgeous for the whole summer,' Elle said. 'And those woven willow fencing panels are great.'

'We wanted to give people a bit of privacy, but we didn't want to use brick walls,' Angie explained.

'Where did you get the panels? I could maybe ask the people who make them to come and give willow weaving classes.'

'I'll find their name for you. They're not far from here—about ten miles.' Angie gave her a sidelong look. 'Charlie could probably give you a lift, if you want to pop over and see them.'

'He won't have the time,' Elle said. 'It's a busy time of year with the animals. I'll just borrow your car, if you don't mind.'

'It's lovely that you're working with him,' Angie said.

Uh-oh. Her mum sounded so hopeful. And Elle was pretty sure she knew where this was leading. Right now, she'd better be cruel to be kind. 'Mum, right now Charlie and I are colleagues. We're becoming friends,' she said. 'But it's never going to be any more than that.' Even though part of her secretly hoped that might change. 'And I'll be back in London at the end of next week.'

'I had hoped,' Angie began, and then she wrinkled her nose. 'Sorry. I'm not trying to manage your life. It's just... I miss you, Ellie. And having you home—it makes the place feel as if the heart's back in it.'

Elle hugged her mother. 'I love you and Dad, Mum. I really do. I'm honestly not trying to avoid you. But my life is in London. It's where I fit.'

'You could fit here,' Angie said. 'Look at all the work you're doing for the farm. There are loads of other local businesses that would love to have your input. You don't have to live in the farmhouse with us; you could have one of the farm cottages, if you'd rather keep your independence.'

'I appreciate the offer, Mum,' Elle said. 'I really appreciate your support, and Dad's. But I'm not staying for ever,' she added, as gently as she could. 'I'm going back to London.'

Her mum was clearly trying to be brave about it, and Elle felt even worse.

'It's not you, Mum. Or Dad. It's me,' she said.

'Is there someone waiting for you in London?'

Elle hugged her again. 'No, Mum. I haven't found the right one, yet.' And she repressed the thought that kissing Charlie, last night, had felt right. Because she and Charlie wanted different things, and there just wasn't room for compromise.

Charlie knew he was going to have to face Elle at some point today—even though it was going to make him squirm. How was he going to manage this? They needed to keep working together; but his feelings towards her weren't colleaguely. If that was even a word. She put his head in such a spin, he couldn't even find the right words for things.

He needed to get over this, fast, for the farm's sake.

Just as he was chugging down his coffee, ready to go out to collect the cows, his phone beeped with a text.

Elle? His heart leaped.

No, of course not. How ridiculous. It could be anyone at all texting him; though it turned out to be Jo, his little sister, checking in before her early-morning dog-walk.

Something you want to tell us, C?

He frowned and texted back.

Sorry, no idea what you mean.

Her reply was a link to a page on the Bluebell Farm website. He clicked on it and groaned; it was the page Elle had tweaked for the shepherd's hut, complete with a collage of the pictures she'd taken last night: the table set for two, the fairy lights giving the inside of the shepherd's hut a romantic air, the food...and a couple of pictures of them together, laughing and drinking bubbles.

He typed back, to explain.

That's Elle. You must remember Mike and Angie's daughter. She was in your year at school. She's revamping the farm's marketing. We're spending the budget on online booking and shopping, and saving money by being the models ourselves.

There was a pause.

If you say so, bro, but the expressions on your faces...

He typed back.

Hey, just nominate us for an acting award. There's nothing going on!

Except Jo had a point. He and Elle *did* look like a real couple. Like two people getting to know each other, being attracted to each other, having a romantic meal together.

He flicked through the website to see what else Elle had done. There were a couple of pictures of flowers, with little snippets of facts he hadn't known: the greater stitchwort's seed capsules made a loud popping when they ripened and fired their seeds, and the plant's name came from its use as a herbal remedy for a stitch, the pain in the side people sometimes felt while out running.

She'd posted more pictures of bluebells, too. *Did you know the bluebell's sticky sap was used to bind the pages of books and to glue feathers onto arrows? In Elizabethan times, the bulbs were crushed to make starch for ruffs. And it takes at least five years for a bluebell seed to develop into a bulb.*

Charlie hadn't known any of that, either. So far, so good. From what he could see, the number of likes on the posts was ticking steadily upwards. They were definitely building an audience.

But then he found the nightingale video. She'd edited it down to thirty seconds of gorgeous song and titled it 'A Nightingale Sang in Bluebell Wood'.

Have you ever heard a nightingale sing? #sweetestsong #soromantic Imagine dancing cheek to cheek in the woods, just the two of you and the nightingale singing and the air full of the scent of bluebells. The sweetest song. The sweetest kiss.

He went hot all over. And for a moment he closed his eyes, remembering how it had felt to dance with her. Remembering how it had felt to smell the vanilla scent of her perfume. The warmth of her skin against his. The way she'd held him close. The way he'd pulled her close, later, when he'd rescued her from falling into the ditch. The way they'd looked at each other in the torchlight, and they'd both leaned in as if some kind of magnet had pulled them together. The way her mouth had felt against his, so sweet and enticing, offering and demanding at the same time.

Even thinking about it made him feel dizzy with a mixture of desire and guilt and pure need.

Had Elle seen his expression on the photograph and interpreted it the same way his sister had? And, if so, just what was he going to do?

He still felt fractious and unsettled when he went to milk the cows. Luckily none of the guests had surfaced early enough to help, so he was free to talk over his thoughts with the cows while he was milking.

'I met her ten years ago. I wouldn't have kissed her then. Apart from the fact that I was dating someone else, that night she was vulnerable,' he said to Elderberry.

The cow lowed softly, as if to encourage him to continue.

He carried on milking and talking. 'She was in tears, for pity's sake. I'd never take advantage of a girl in distress. Besides, she was the same age as my little sister. Way too young for me.'

Elderberry mooed, as if to point out that the three-year age gap didn't matter any more, now that he was thirty-one and she was twenty-eight.

'I know the farm needs a shake-up in the marketing. Her ideas are great. But this romantic narrative thing…it's getting too complicated.'

Elderberry swished her tail, as if to say, 'Nonsense.'

'I kissed her last night.' He sighed. 'It wasn't meant to happen. She slipped, and I grabbed her before she fell in the mud, and…it just felt natural for her to be in my arms. Especially because we'd danced together, earlier. And then I kissed her.' He leaned his forehead against Elderberry's flank. 'One kiss wasn't enough. The next thing I knew, she was kissing me back. And it was perfect.'

Elderberry's next moo was very clearly the bovine version of, *So what happened next?*

'An owl hooted. It brought us to our senses. We broke apart, and we both said it was an accident.' He switched buckets. 'Except I wasn't telling the truth. I wanted to kiss her again. I still do. Even though I know it's a bad idea.'

Another swish of her tail.

'It's a *really* bad idea, Elderberry. I'm not going to offer her a fling—that's not who I am. But how can I offer her anything more? She doesn't want to stay here, and I don't want to go to London. There isn't a way to compromise. Besides, she's the daughter of my business partners. I don't want to make things complicated. I *like* living here. I'm happy.'

As he said it, he realised to his surprise that he was.

He missed Jess and he still felt hollow, without her; but working with the animals and the land had helped to heal the rawness of that loss. Now, he could enjoy his daily routine, noticing the changes in the plants and the animals. He could find pleasure in watching a lamb bouncing about in the fields or the cows kicking up their heels as they went into new pasture. He could appreciate the sight of a fairy ring of mushrooms appearing overnight, the sound of rich birdsong heralding the dawn, the scent of woodland flowers as he walked the land, the rich taste of the cheese made on the farm from the cows he'd milked with his own hands.

What was missing was *touch*.

He'd coped without it until Elle had held him close and kissed him back. Her touch had been like water on a parched flower, letting his feelings bloom—and now he wanted more. He wanted *her*.

'I really don't know how to fix this, Elderberry,' he said to the cow as he finished milking her, put the milk out of the way and made a fuss of her.

She licked his face.

'It's not as easy as that,' he said.

She licked him again, her sandpapery tongue telling him that he was making too big a deal about it and he just needed to talk to Elle.

'It isn't,' he repeated.

Another lick.

'I'll think about it,' he promised.

Somehow he'd find a way to get back on an even keel with Elle—and keep his feelings completely under control. But, until he'd sorted his head out, he thought it might be a good idea to avoid her.

When Elle had finished helping her mum, she visited Rosie on the other side of town and had a wonderful time learning to card and spin wool, as well as making a fuss of Rosie's sheep. And she was delighted when Rosie agreed to run a class on dyeing yarn as well as helping with a weekly craft session in the café.

She checked her emails in the car, and was thrilled to see that Frieda had sent four potential logos. There was one that particularly stood out for her, but this wasn't her decision. She'd need to discuss it with her parents.

And with Charlie.

She sighed. OK, so it had been awkward between them since that kiss. She'd pretty much avoided him this morning, and she was pretty sure that he'd been avoiding her in exactly the same way. But, if she was going to do this job professionally, she needed to move past that kiss and work with Charlie. Particularly as they didn't have much time to get the media stuff up and running.

Maybe the best way forward was to pretend that the kiss hadn't happened. Keep it brisk and businesslike.

She flicked into her messaging app.

Hi. Discussed classes with Rosie and just had logo drafts from Frieda. When are you free to discuss farm website? Thanks, E

Elle had just parked the car back at the farm when her phone pinged with a message.

Free at 3. My kitchen? Will have kettle on. C

She only realised how tense she'd been when she leaned back against the seat. He wasn't going to make it difficult. He, too, was clearly going to pretend that kiss hadn't happened.

Good.

She texted back.

3 works for me.

She called into the café to see her mum and Lisa, and arranged to observe her mum's cheese-making class, the following day; then she mocked up four versions of the home page for the farm's website, using the different logos.

The butterflies in her stomach grew restless again as she walked to Charlie's cottage with her laptop. Would she get away with pretending that kiss hadn't happened, or would he bring it up? And, if he did… What then?

Was he trying to persuade himself that he didn't want to repeat it, the way she was? Did he want her to keep her distance? Or had he found a way where they could compromise?

There was a knock on the kitchen door at exactly three o'clock.

Elle.

Keep it cool and calm, Charlie reminded himself, and went to answer the door.

She was dressed casually, in jeans and a T-shirt and canvas shoes, with a lime-green satchel slung over her shoulder. He wished she'd been wearing her fancy London clothes instead, because the formal dress made her look much less approachable. As it was, he itched to pull her into his arms again and kiss her until they were both dizzy.

Not happening, he reminded himself, and he knew he sounded grumpy when he asked, 'Did you want coffee?' He just hoped she'd put it down to anything but the truth. Anything but the fact that he was crazily attracted to a woman who didn't want the same things out of life that he did and it would never, ever work between them.

She acted as if he'd been perfectly sweet and pleasant towards her. 'Coffee would be lovely, thank you, Charlie.'

Oh, the way his name sounded on her mouth. He wanted to make her groan it in pleasure. To scream it in joy.

He didn't dare close his eyes, because then he'd see the pictures in his head even more clearly. Think of mucking out the byre, he told himself. Think of cleaning things. Think of anything except Eleanor Newton and her lush, perfect Cupid's bow of a mouth.

'Take a seat.' He gestured to the kitchen table and went to make coffee, hoping that the activity would give him the space for his common sense to kick back in.

By the time he brought the two mugs over to the table, she'd taken her laptop out of the satchel and switched it on. 'Frieda's sent me four logos. I've done a mock-up of the new home page, but I wanted to run things by you, first. I've also written a few blog posts, which we can schedule in for the next few weeks.'

'I saw the one on bluebells,' he said. 'I learned a lot—and I like the way you write.'

She went pink. 'Thank you.'

She'd looked as pink as that when the owl had interrupted their kiss. All flushed and dewy and delectable.

Then he realised he'd missed what she'd said. 'Sorry. Could you repeat that, please?'

'We need to talk about tags. What people are likely to search for. Cows, flowers, recipes...'

'Right.'

Where did he sit?

Opposite her felt too intimate.

At right angles to her meant he risked accidentally touching her, which would also be too intimate. Even the thought of her skin brushing against his made his blood feel as if it were fizzing in his veins.

How the hell did he feel so off kilter and out of place in his own home?

And it shook him to realise that, actually, this *was* home. The cottage might not belong to him, but he belonged there.

Completely flustered—and knowing that Elle was the cause of said flusterment—Charlie put the mugs of coffee on the table and took the chair at right angles to hers.

She moved her laptop so he could see the screen. 'These are Frieda's four suggestions.'

Simple, clear lettering—Bluebell Farm—with an equally simple line-drawing of bluebells. He studied them, trying to ignore just how close Elle's hand was to his own. 'I really like this one, where she's turned the F of farm into a bluebell,' he said.

'That's my favourite, too,' she said. 'I think it'd work really well on the website, on leaflets, and on labels. Black lettering, with just the bluebell in blue. As soon as people see that flower, they'll think of us. But,' she added, 'obviously Mum and Dad need to be on board with it.'

'I'm sure they will be.' He could keep himself focused on business. Even if his head was full of pictures of Elle lying on a picnic rug, laughing up at him, with the remains of a punnet of strawberries between them and her lips stained with strawberry juice as he'd fed them to her one by one...

'Yup,' he mumbled. Oh, dear God. No, he wasn't functioning as if this was a business meeting. He'd never even been like this with Jess. What the hell was going on with his head?

'Rosie's agreed to run a class on dyeing yarn and help with a knitting hour.' She grinned. 'And I had a go at spinning wool today.'

Wool was a neutral topic. He seized on it gratefully. 'So how did it go?'

'She showed me loads of the different staples—that's a length of wool, to you, and how long it is differs by the breed of sheep—and how you card it to make sure all the fibres go the same way. Actually, she uses a dog comb because it's easier. And you wouldn't believe how soft camel hair is.'

'Camel hair?' he repeated. This was surreal.

'People knit with camel hair and goat hair,' Elle said. 'Even dog hair.'

'And that's what you're suggesting people do here?'

Her smile sparkled with mischief. 'That might be a bit *too* way out. But I love the idea of people working with wool from our sheep. I had a go with a drop spindle. It's amazing to think that for millennia women have taken a piece of fluffy wool, used a drop spindle to turn it into yarn, then woven it into cloth,' she said. 'It really connects you with the past.'

He had a feeling that she was going to write a blog all about it. A feeling that deepened when she showed him photos of herself grinning widely as she spun the drop spindle and the yarn began to form. 'Right.' Focus, for pity's sake, he told himself. On something other than how easy it would be to lean over and kiss Elle again. 'So, the spinning: was it easy?'

'No,' she admitted. 'I found it really hard to hold the fleece right and tease it out. But then I had a go on the spinning wheel. And that...' Her smile broadened. 'It's like learning to drive again and having to do several things at once when you've never done one of them before—using the treadle to keep the wheel moving, drawing out the fleece and feeding it into the wheel, keeping the tension even so the spun wool's spaced evenly on the spindle. It's like steering and changing gear and indicating and checking your road position and everything round you all at the same time, for the very first time.'

He had a feeling that he was going to enjoy reading more of her blog posts.

'And then—' she paused dramatically '—there's the niddy-noddy.'

'The *what*?' Surely she'd made that word up?

'Niddy-noddy,' she repeated. 'It's a wooden thing and you wind the wool round it to make a skein.' She pulled up some photos of herself winding wool around a wooden instrument that reminded him a bit of a mug-tree. 'See?'

'You've made the name up, right?'

'No. There are two possible etymologies. I was going to do a poll to see what the most popular one is.'

'And you're going to leave it there?'

'I could,' she teased.

This version of Elle was irresistible. If she carried on like this, he'd need to sit on his hands to stop himself pulling her into his arms. Except that would be too obvious. He crossed his arms, hoping that she would think he was being grumpy rather than realising that he was protecting himself. 'But you're not going to.'

'OK. The first one is that the name comes from the nodding motion made as you wind the wool.'

He'd just bet that the second explanation was better.

'Or,' she said, 'it's because winding the wool into skein was usually done by an elderly granny, known as a "niddy". That, plus the motion of winding the wool… Isn't that *delicious*?'

She was delicious. Her enthusiasm brightened up his day. Unable to say a word, he just nodded.

She laughed. 'Excellent response. Oh, and just so you know, they've been used for centuries. Two niddy-noddies were found in a Viking ship burial of two women in Norway, along with other weaving equipment. There are pictures in medieval manuscripts. And even Leonardo da Vinci painted one in his "Madonna of the Yarnwinder".'

'You're going to write a blog post about a niddy-noddy, aren't you?'

'Along with a video of Rosie demonstrating how to use one,' she said. 'Want to see the skein I made?' She drew a bundle out of her pocket. 'Rosie started me off. That's this bit which is all even and lovely.' She threw one hand out in a 'ta-da' gesture. 'And this bit is mine.'

The yarn was thin and twisted to the point where it curled back over itself in some places, and fluffy with thick blobs in others. It looked utterly hopeless, but he didn't want to squash her enthusiasm. He didn't know what to say.

'I know, I know—I think it's absolutely terrible, too,' she said, still laughing. 'Though Rosie said it was good for a very first attempt, and if I did the full class I'd get the hang of it. But feel how soft the wool is.'

Bad move. It made him think about how soft her skin was. How much he wanted to kiss her…

But they were already in trouble over that. And he needed to tell her about it.

'My sister texted me, this morning,' he said. 'About the post you put up.'

'The bluebells?'

'The shepherd's huts.'

She smiled. 'I was pleased with that. We did a good job between us.'

'Yeah, but Jo thought we were dating.'

She stilled. 'What did you say to her?' Her voice was filled with wariness.

'That she could nominate us for an award.'

'Because we're acting a part,' Elle said. 'Good save.' She drained her mug. 'I'd better let you get on. I'll wash this up first.'

'No need,' he said.

'OK. I'll let you know what Mum and Dad say about the logo.' She gave him a smile he could only describe as tight, and left the kitchen.

What had he said?

He thought about it. Was she upset because Jo had thought they were dating, or because he'd been so quick to refute the suggestion?

Asking her bluntly would open a massive can of worms. He needed to think about a better way of broaching the subject. Particularly as he was still torn over the whole idea of dating again and moving on. He knew it was something he needed to do, but it was so hard.

Charlie was working in the woods, an hour later, when he saw the swans at the pool with their cygnets.

Despite the slight awkwardness between them, he knew Elle wouldn't want to miss this.

He called her. 'Can you spare five minutes—and I mean as in can you come here right this very second?'

'Ye-es. Why?'

'You'll see when you get here. If your phone battery's low, you can use mine.'

'Where exactly are you?' she asked, sounding intrigued.

'By the pond in the woods.' He knew he didn't need to be more specific. She knew the land.

'Be there in five,' she said.

He took some video of the swans and cygnets, just in case they'd gone by the time she arrived; but then he heard someone walking towards him. Funny how he didn't even need to turn round to know it was her rather than someone else; his spine was tingling, his skin felt tight, and his breathing had gone all shallow.

'What was so urg—? Ohh,' she said, seeing the swans.

He loved the way her face lit up with pleasure, her dark eyes shimmering with joy.

'Thank you for sharing this with me,' she said as she flicked into her camera app. 'Aren't they gorgeous?' She filmed the cygnets as they paddled across the lake between their mum at the front of the line and their dad at the rear; the cygnets were peeping madly, as if to say, 'Hurry up, Dad!'

Finally, the swan family came to a stop and climbed out onto the bank of the pool, where they sat in the dappled sunlight.

'That was absolutely amazing,' she said. 'Thank you for sharing it with me.'

'I knew you'd love it as much as I did. Do you miss this side of the farm?' he asked, taking a risk because he thought that bringing up the subject might send her rushing away again.

She lifted one shoulder. 'There are swans in London as well as in the country, you know. Kensington Park, Bushy Park—and there are black swans at St James's Park.'

Of course there were. He'd seen them himself, in the years when he'd lived in London. But he thought she might be protesting just a little bit too much, and he was glad that—even if she didn't admit it—she was starting to see the good side of the farm again.

'Mum and Dad agreed with you about the logo, by the way, so I've asked Frieda to do me the final artwork. I've touched base with the agency, and the techy team tells me the booking system for accommodation, classes and lunch is ready for testing, but we still need to do a bit of work on packaging and handling the shipping of perishables before we can test the farm shop system.'

'I salute your organisational skills,' he said.

She grinned. 'I'm the scary one in the office—the one who's always talking about critical path analysis.'

'So what else do we need to do on the wedding side?'

'A picture of our couple with a romantic sunset and a romantic sunrise, one or both also being with the wildflower meadow in the background,' she said.

'Sunset would be better for the meadow. Hang on a second.' He checked the weather forecast. 'Sunrise tomorrow is at half-past five. Are you up for being out in the fields at five o'clock? Because that way we'll get all the gorgeous colours just before the sun comes up.'

'Wide Norfolk skies looking like a watercolour. That's one of the things I miss, in London,' she said.

'It's a—' He stopped himself before the d-word came out of his mouth. 'Plan,' he said instead. 'And now I'd better let you get on.'

'I'll plan the other shots I need,' she said. 'Including video of cows playing football and lambs gambolling, oh and us cuddling lambs.'

'And we need photos of Brick,' he said.

'Brick?'

'The Suffolk Punch who arrives here next week with Eddie—his best friend's a donkey,' he reminded her. 'If our wedding parties want it, Brick will pull the carriage.'

'What carriage?'

'It's at the local college at the moment. I have a friend who teaches woodwork, and his students—apprentices, really—are restoring it for me,' he said, and flicked into the photos app of his phone. 'This is what it looked like last year.'

'Are you quite sure that's a carriage and not a heap of firewood?' she asked.

He smiled. 'Our apprentices have fixed the wheels, mended the carriage and painted it white, and they're working on the upholstery and the convertible hood. Imagine arriving to your wedding in this, pulled by a Suffolk Punch whose coat has been burnished to a bright sheen and his mane and tail braided.' He showed her the most recent photograph of the carriage.

'That's gorgeous,' she said. 'Can I have more information on the carriage restoration? Because I think this is the sort of thing people would be really interested in. And photographs. Including the apprentices, if they'll sign a release for me. That's really heartwarming. From firewood to...' She looked thoughtful. 'I'll work on the headline for the press release.'

'OK. I'll send them over to you tonight and check with the lecturers. See you tomorrow at five for the sunrise,' he said.

She smiled at him, her expression much warmer and, to his relief, without the wariness she'd exhibited this afternoon. 'See you tomorrow at five, outside your place.'

CHAPTER SEVEN

ON FRIDAY, Elle met Charlie at his kitchen door.
He had a waterproof rug over one arm and was
carrying two travel mugs of coffee, one of which
he gave to her.

'Nicely prepared,' she said. 'I didn't even think
about coffee; I was focusing on the photographs.'

He laughed. 'Nice pun, Ms Newton.'

'Sadly, it was unintentional.' She laughed
back at him.

The sky was still pale blue when they reached
the spot Charlie had mentioned yesterday. 'So
much for a sky full of colour,' she said, disappointed.

'At least we've got the dawn chorus,' he reminded her.

'So it's worth taking a bit of video as well
as stills. Good point,' she said. She took some
video of the birds singing, then settled down on
the blanket next to him. She shivered. 'It's a bit
colder than I expected.'

'Maybe we need to share some body heat.' He shifted closer and put his arm round her. 'Better?'

'Better,' she said, though the warmth blooming through her wasn't just because of his body heat: it was because of him. She knew he was doing this solely because he was a nice guy, and she needed to tamp down the fizzy feelings of pleasure because they weren't a real couple. He was her fake boyfriend, soon to be fake fiancé, and they were doing this simply to help sell the idea of holding a wedding at Bluebell Farm.

The sky gradually turned lilac and the top edge of the sun appeared at the far end of the fields, a deep rich pink in colour.

'That's stunning. What a colour!' She took an array of shots as the sun rose steadily. 'With those wisps of cloud across it, it looks as stripy as Jupiter.'

'It's fantastic,' he agreed. 'Sights like these make it worth getting up earlier than I need to for milking.'

'Do you want me to give you a hand this morning?' she asked.

'If you have time,' he said.

She thoroughly enjoyed helping bring the cows in, then milking them by hand and taking the covered buckets of milk through to the dairy barn next door.

'I'm doing Mum's dairy class today,' she said. 'I could bring the cheese over and make us a pasta dinner.'

'Or we could cook together,' he suggested. You bring the pasta or whatever, and I'll sort the pudding and the wine.'

It felt quite like a date, but Charlie had already made it clear he didn't think of her in that way. 'OK. I'll take more pics of a romantic meal, if you don't mind.'

'Just as well my kitchen's tidy,' he grumbled.

'Otherwise I would've made you clean it,' she said.

'So bossy.' He rolled his eyes. 'I thought the client was supposed to be the boss?'

'The client agreed the brief,' she said sweetly, 'so now I'm in charge.'

He laughed. 'Got it. See you later.'

Elle spent the morning doing her mum's class, picked up what she wanted for the rest of the main course from the farm shop, and did some more work on the farm's website before heading over to Charlie's.

'So what are we cooking?' he asked.

'Gnocchi alla Sorrentina,' she said. 'I cooked the potatoes at Mum's, just to save a bit of time.'

'We're making the gnocchi?'

'It's really easy. Potato and flour. My best friend's vegan, so I tend to use olive oil rather than egg. And I'm assuming you don't have a potato ricer, so I've borrowed Mum's.'

'Potato ricer?'

She took the gadget out of her bag and waved it at him. 'You'll enjoy this,' she promised.

And it was immense fun, teaching him how to make gnocchi and how to roll the balls of dough down the tines of a fork to get the little ridges on one side and photographing him doing it. She made the tomato, basil and mozzarella sauce while the gnocchi cooked, then added the gnocchi to the sauce, topped it with more mozzarella and slid it into the oven.

'Twenty minutes. So we have time to clear up first,' she said.

'I feel a bit guilty that I completely cheated with pudding,' he said. 'I bought berries, ice cream and shortbread from the farm shop.'

'No complaints from me,' she said, smiling.

By the time they'd finished clearing up, the gnocchi was ready.

'This is delicious,' he said. 'This is the cheese you made with your mum, this morning?'

'Yes. Mozzarella-style. We've got some Brie maturing as well. I might need you to take photos of the finished product when I'm back in London,' she said.

It was the first time ever that she could remember not quite looking forward to going back to London. Though that was ridiculous. London was where she belonged, not here.

She pushed the thoughts away and chatted with Charlie over dinner, then curled up in a corner of his sofa with a glass of red wine and music playing in the background.

'I was impressed by the way you could heft a full pail of milk, this morning,' he said.

She rolled her eyes at him. 'I already told you I lift weights in the gym. Fifteen litres of milk is nothing.' She smiled. 'I love the gym. It clears my head after work and lets me wind down. I do classes mainly, with my best friend: Zumba, dance aerobics, and spin, and sometimes Pilates on a Sunday morning.'

'You're not a runner, then?'

She shook her head. 'I loathe steady state cardio, except spin class. My weights routines are all HIIT, because otherwise I get bored.' She looked at him. 'I'm guessing you don't bother with the gym, because you get all the exercise you need on the farm.'

'A lot of walking, a bit of lifting—it's enough to make me hot and sweaty,' he agreed.

She thought of what else would make them hot and sweaty, and her temperature rose a degree.

'Did you go to the gym when you lived in London?' she asked.

'I used to go before work,' he said. 'I did weights, and intervals on the rowing machine.'

'You're not a runner, either, then?'

'No, but I've been thinking lately I'd like a dog to walk around the farm with me,' he admitted.

'The farm doesn't feel quite right without a dog,' she said. 'When we lost our Honey, it was when Gran was really ill, and Dad said it was the wrong time to get a puppy. And then, later, he said we were all too busy to have time for a pup.' She shrugged. 'I guess he had a point.'

'You miss having a dog?'

'Yes, but it wouldn't be fair to have a dog in London. Not with the hours I work. She'd be left on her own all the time. Not like here, where you could take your dog to work with you.'

'True.' He paused. 'I've been thinking. The last pictures we need to do are dressing the barn for a wedding, and the "engagement". How are we going to manage that?'

'Gran left me her engagement ring. We could use that for the "engagement" pictures.' She looked at him. 'Are you sure you're OK about this?'

'Surprisingly, yes. You've made it feel less…' He shook his head. 'I can't find the right words. Less like being sucked into the middle of a black hole, I guess.'

'I'm glad.'

'I have a day off, tomorrow. It's meant to be sunny, so we could go to the beach, if you like.'

'And make sandcastles—we need to show that the farm is great for families, as well as for romantic breaks. Maybe we could go to Wells-next-the-Sea? I haven't been there since...' She shook her head. 'I can't remember when. But sometimes Dad would bundle us all into the car, including Honey, and we'd walk the whole length of the beach from Wells to Holkham before going back to the café for hot chocolate and some cake.'

'Wells it is,' he said.

It was a perfect day when Charlie drove them to the beach; the sky was the deep blue of early summer with fluffy white clouds scudding across, and it was warm enough not to need a coat.

Elle said, 'It's such a treat to come to the beach. That's something else I miss in London. I've been to Brighton, but the beach is all pebbly and it's not like having acres of golden sand to walk on.'

Charlie took two bamboo cups out of the back of the car. 'The beach is even more of a treat with coffee.'

People were already seated at the wooden

tables outside the beach café with their dogs, enjoying the sunshine; Elle couldn't resist stopping to make a fuss of a golden Labrador pup, and by the time she joined Charlie inside he'd already bought the coffee—and, to her amusement, buckets and spades.

'Seriously? You actually bought buckets and spades?'

'You said you wanted pictures of sandcastles,' he reminded her, 'and if we just use our hands the sandcastles are going to be pretty feeble.'

'You're right. Thank you for remembering.'

He shrugged off the compliment, but he looked faintly pleased.

Even though there were quite a few cars in the car park, the beach was long enough and wide enough for them to have plenty of space.

'When does the tide come back in?' she asked, remembering that the tide rushed in quite quickly on this part of the coast.

'Early evening. We don't have to hurry,' he said.

She rolled up her jeans to her knees and took off her shoes, enjoying the feel of wet sand beneath her feet.

'You're seriously going to paddle in the North Sea when it's only just May?' he asked.

'It's glorious,' she said. 'The rush of the waves as they come tumbling in, and the swishing as the water trickles back out.' She looked pointedly at his feet. 'Or are you too chicken to join me?'

'I'm fine as I am. I'll look after your shoes and your coffee,' he said, and sat on the sand with his arms wrapped round his knees.

'Your choice,' she said, and went to paddle at the edge of the sea.

This was where her fiancé would play in the waves next to her, scooping her up in his arms and pretending to drop her into the water. Where she'd shriek and he'd laugh and then he'd kiss her...

Except she and Charlie weren't an item.

And maybe this hadn't been a great idea.

If he'd loved going to the beach with Jess, this must be bringing back memories for him—and with memories would come the emptiness of loss.

Guilt flooded through her, and she went back to join him. 'You OK?' she asked.

'Yes. Why?'

'It was your idea to come here,' she said, 'but you're not paddling in the sea and you look as if you're a million miles away, in your head.' She took his hand and squeezed it briefly. 'I'm assuming Jess loved the sea.'

'She did,' he said. 'We honeymooned in St Lucia, and it was amazing—cobalt sea, whit sands, and the volcanos rising up. We did a bit of exploring while we were there: hiking through the rainforest, visiting waterfalls, and on one day we actually drove into a volcano and walked round the sulphur pools.' He smiled. 'It takes a while to get the mud off your skin, though. We used to sit and watch the sun setting over the sea every night. And we went during hatchling season, so there was one night when we went to see the turtles. It's humbling, watching hundreds and hundreds of these tiny creatures flippering their way across the sand towards the sea.'

'That sounds amazing,' she said. 'Is that what made you decide to do your Masters in Environmental Studies, seeing the turtles and the rainforest?'

'It was probably one of the seeds,' he said. 'I just knew I wanted to make a difference. To make the world a better place.'

'And you're doing exactly that,' she said. 'I never knew your Jess, but I'd just bet she's up there right now, beaming down, really proud of you and what you're doing at Bluebell Farm.'

'You might well be right.' He paused. 'Funny, you're the only person I can really talk to about her.'

'Probably because I never knew her,' she said. 'So it's not like it must be with her family and friends, when you'd be trying to spare their feelings or worry that you're trampling over their grief.'

'I appreciate it,' he said, lacing his fingers through hers. 'I appreciate *you*.'

Her skin was tingling where he touched her. 'I appreciate you, too,' she said. More than appreciated him. It would be very easy to let herself fall in love with Charlie Webb. But, with her track record in men, she knew it wouldn't work out. Better to leave things as they were. 'Now I think it's time to regress a quarter of a century and make sandcastles. I challenge you to make a better one than me.' She gently disengaged her fingers from his and set the alarm on her phone. 'We've got ten minutes. Starting…now!'

Armed with a bucket and spade each, they shovelled sand into the buckets to build towers, and dug moats. Charlie didn't start a conversation, clearly concentrating on building his sandcastle; but, to Elle's relief, his expression wasn't quite as bleak as it had been earlier.

'Five minutes to decorate them and fill the moats,' she said when the alarm went off.

When the second alarm went off, she'd just finished making windows in her towers with shells.

'All right. Let judgement commence,' she said. Being rude about his castle was probably the best way to get him to tease her back and finish getting him out of his bleak mood. 'Castle Webb has five towers, because her builder is showing off. It has a moat, but no drawbridge, and no door or windows. Plus I assume that bit of seaweed on a twig is meant to be some kind of pennant?'

'It's *obviously* a pennant,' he said. 'And it looks like a web so it's a visual representation of the name.'

'It doesn't look anything like a web,' she scoffed. 'Any spider making *that* would have to be drunk.'

'Let's have a look at Castle Newton,' he said. 'Four towers, because her builder is being super-traditional and boring. No pennant, so the castle could belong to absolutely anyone.'

'Yeah, but there's a drawbridge over my moat,' she said, indicating the razor clam shells, 'and a doorway, and windows. I win.'

'No way. That's just girly showing-off,' Charlie pronounced.

What could she do but upend the bucket of seawater over him instead of pouring it into her moat?

He stared at her, looking utterly shocked— and then did exactly the same thing to her.

'Sauce for the goose,' he said when she gasped in outrage.

'We don't have geese on the farm—and neither of us would eat the goose, anyway,' she pointed out.

'True,' he admitted. 'Even though you soaked me first, I apologise.'

'You don't look in the slightest bit sorry,' she said.

'Neither do you,' he retorted.

'I'm not. I'm planning a second ambush.'

'You're playing a dangerous game, there,' he said. 'Because I could pick you up, carry you to the sea and drop you in.'

'In which case I'd take your legs out from under you,' she said, 'so you'd end up just as wet. Do you have a change of clothes in the car, or even a towel?'

'Um…no,' he admitted. 'Perhaps we should both call a truce.'

'Admit my shell windows are pretty, first.'

He folded his arms. 'Only if you admit my pennant is genius.'

She beckoned him closer. He bent his head slightly so she could whisper into his ear. 'It's pants.'

'The truce is off,' he said, and to her shock he picked her up.

'No. No. Charlie! You wouldn't!' she shrieked as he strode over to the sea.

'Say it. The pennant is genius,' he demanded.

'It's a bit of seaweed on a twig.' She coughed. 'You say it. The shells are pretty.'

'They *match*. It's meant to be a sandcastle, Elle. You're supposed to use the first shells you find.'

'That's *so* blokey,' she retorted.

He was standing in the sea, now, and the water was up to mid-calf. 'Did I hear the word "genius"?'

'You absolutely did not.' The way he was carrying her meant that she couldn't wrap her legs round him, but she could cling on to his neck. 'Say "pretty shells".'

'Nope.'

'Drop me, and I'll make sure you're soaked,' she warned.

'Am I meant to be scared?'

'Yeah, you are. I'm Elle Newton. Everyone knows I deliver on my promises,' she said.

'You do indeed,' he said.

She'd fantasised about her fake fiancé doing precisely this, but the reality was something else.

Charlie Webb was utterly gorgeous. Those blue, blue eyes that sparkled brighter than the ocean. His hair, still wet from the seawater she'd tipped over his head, was slicked back and starting to curl as it dried, making him look like the Greek god of the sea. She was no lightweight,

but he'd carried her down the beach with p
fect ease. And his mouth, curved into a te
ing smile, was beautiful. She wanted to p
his head down to hers and kiss him until th
were both dizzy.

He was staring at her mouth, too, as if he w
thinking exactly the same thing. That she w
some nymph of the sea, one of the Sirens, a
he was a sailor driven to distraction by her so

Just when she was convinced that he w
going to follow through on his threat and d
her into the sea, instead he lowered her saf
to the ground.

Her arms were still round his neck, and
the life of her she couldn't let him go. He sta
at her, his tongue moistening his lower
and her control snapped. She pulled his h
down to hers and kissed him. His mouth v
warm and sweet, and she wanted more. Pre
ing closer, she nibbled at his lower lip until
opened his mouth and let her deepen the ki

His body was hard and muscular against h
and the muscles were all from hard work rat
than being honed in a gym. Charlie Webb m
her head spin. And she'd never wanted any
so badly in her l—

She pulled away from him and shrieked
cold seawater splashed all over her.

A chocolate Labrador, a tennis ball in

mouth, was bounding through the shallows and showering them with water.

'Sorry!' the owner called, looking mortified.

'That's OK!' she called back.

It was probably just as well that the cold water had brought them both back to their senses. Who knew what that kiss might have led to?

'I'm sorry. I shouldn't have done that,' she said.

'I shouldn't have kissed you back, either,' he said, flushing scarlet.

'Let's pretend that didn't happen,' she said.

'Except it did,' he said. 'Twice. And I think, if we're both honest, we both want it to happen again.'

All the breath went out of her lungs and she couldn't say a word.

'Elle?'

'Yeah,' she managed eventually. 'It's the same for me.'

'So what are we going to do about it?'

He was braver than her, asking that. So she owed it to him to be honest. 'I'm going back to London in a week. My life's there, not here. And I...' She blew out a breath. 'My relationships have all been disasters. Right from what I thought was a prom date with Damien Price—and of *course* the most popular boy in school didn't want to go to prom with me.'

* * *

'The hurt from that night really went deep, didn't it?' Charlie asked.

'I'm not sure what hurt more,' she said. 'The fact that everyone except me knew it was fake, or the fact that Damien thought I'd be so grateful to be asked that I'd do absolutely anything he wanted.'

Charlie threaded his fingers through hers again. 'Damien Price was an immature, callous little boy. The blame's on him, not you.'

'Is it, though?' she asked. 'Because why do I always pick men who seem perfect, and then when they see where I come from they can't back away fast enough?'

'I'm no psychologist,' he said. 'I can't help you find an answer to that.' He paused. 'But I see where you come from. And it doesn't make me want to run.'

'Because you bought into it. It's your dream,' she said. 'And it's my nightmare.'

'Is it, though?' Charlie asked, echoing her earlier question. 'Because, this last week, I've seen you throw yourself into helping make the farm work.'

'It's my job,' she said, 'and you know I've got a promotion riding on the campaign being a success. Plus it's for my parents. And—' She stopped.

And for him? Charlie wondered. Or for the farm itself? Her drew her hand up to his lips and kissed each knuckle in turn. 'What if,' he said, 'this thing between you and me isn't just… I dunno, propinquity?'

'That's not a farming term. Or a banking one.'

'And that's not an answer,' he retorted. 'I like you, Elle Newton. I like you a lot.'

'And I like you,' she admitted.

'You're the first woman I've kissed—the first woman I've *wanted* to kiss—since Jess.'

'But every time we kiss, we get interrupted. The rooster. The owl. The dog who splashed us just now. Maybe Nature's trying to tell us something. That we shouldn't be together.'

'Running scared, Elle?'

'No—yes.' She wrinkled her nose. 'You asked me once about my five-year plan. I told you what I wanted. Promotion, and then eventually running my own agency. In London.' She looked him straight in the eyes. 'So if this thing between you and me becomes more of a thing— would you be prepared to move back to London to be with me?'

'Would you move back to the farm to be with me?' he countered.

'That's a question, not an answer,' she said. 'Or maybe it *is* an answer. The same as mine.

No. I admit, you're right in that it's changed since I was a teenager. But this isn't London. London's what I want.' She brought their joined hands to her mouth and copied his earlier actions, kissing each knuckle in turn. 'I don't think it'd be fair to either of us to have a fling. It'd get messy. We need to agree to be friends, and keep it there.'

'Friends,' he said. 'I'd like us to be more— and I'm not saying that to guilt you into doing what I want. The sensible side of me knows that you're absolutely right.' He wasn't quite ready to relinquish her hand. 'Just for the record, Damien and the rest of the Mr Wrongs were completely clueless. You're special, Elle. And you deserve someone who not only accepts where you come from, but backs you all the way and helps you get your dreams.'

Her gorgeous dark eyes glittered with tears. 'You're special, too, Charlie. And you deserve someone who'll love you and who'll love the farm as much as you do.'

He dropped her hand so he could put his arms round her, then held her close. She was the most stubborn woman he'd ever met. But he'd back off now, for her sake. 'Right, Ms Newton.' He released her and took a step back. 'We're skiving off, and we have a job to do—taking pictures for the farm. Of our fake—*acting*,' he corrected, 'fiancé and fiancée. What did you have in mind?'

'An open ring box on top of a castle,' she said.

'Castle Webb,' he said immediately.

She scoffed. 'Castle Newton's way more photogenic.'

'And it's very girly. Nobody's going to believe that your fiancé made something like that,' he pointed out.

'I suppose you have a point,' she admitted.

'So the narrative is—I built a castle, you went to get water to fill the moat, and came back to find the box on top of the castle?'

'That works,' she said. 'I guess you ought to see the ring.' She took the box from her pocket and opened it. 'It was my grandmother's.'

'It's really pretty,' he said. 'So is this what you'll wear when you eventually get engaged?'

'No,' she said. 'In London, I wear this most days on my right hand.'

'What sort of engagement ring would you like?'

She narrowed her eyes, clearly thinking about it. 'I think one of those *toi-et-moi* rings.'

'You and me,' he translated. 'One stone for you, and one for your fiancé?'

'Yes. A tanzanite, because it's the colour of the bluebells at home, and a pink sapphire heart.'

He wondered if she'd realised the significance of what she'd just said: she'd described a ring that would be so important to her, and she'd chosen a stone to remind her of where she'd grown up. The place she'd once loved…

She'd said that her life was in London now, but he'd seen her all lit up at the farm when she was with the animals and the flowers and the sunrise. She'd admitted that she didn't hate it here, the way she had as a teen. So maybe he just needed to be patient. Wait for her to see it for herself: to realise that maybe she could learn to love it again. Could learn to love *him*.

She set the open box on the top of his sand-castle, and took a snap.

'There's something missing,' he said.

'What?'

'Water for the moat.' And something else. Which he probably shouldn't do, but it was irresistible. 'Off you go. Two buckets.' He made shooing motions in the direction of the sea

Charlie could've fetched the water himself, Elle thought crossly. On the other hand, maybe he'd done it deliberately to give her some space, because thinking about her grandmother and the bluebell woods had made her all wistful.

When she came back, she saw the words written in the wet sand by the moat. *Marry me?*

For a moment, it felt real. As if he'd actually proposed to her. Wanted to spend his life with her. Wanted to build a future with her.

She couldn't breathe, and her knees had turned to sea-foam.

But then a dog barked in the distance, and reality swooped back in. Of course Charlie didn't want to marry her. This was window-dressing for the farm website. Nothing more.

He didn't want her to shriek with excitement, fling her arms round him and say yes.

'Nice touch,' she said. 'And I like the fact you punctuated it properly. A question rather than a demand.' She risked a very quick glance and was relieved to see that she'd struck the right tone.

'I wouldn't have dared to do otherwise,' he said. 'Otherwise you'd have lambasted me about my rubbish grammar and made me write it out correctly a hundred times.'

'I might've let you off with twenty,' she said lightly. 'Can you pour the water in the moat for me? I don't want it to vanish into the sand before I can take the picture. And you need to be on this side so there's no shadow.'

'Sure. I'll count you down. Three, two, one, water,' he said, and poured the first bucket in.

'Perfect,' she said, 'Thank you.' She showed him the snap, the water in the moat glittering in the sunlight almost as much as the ring on top of the castle.

'Our target audience would expect to see the ring on the third finger of your left hand,' he said.

She winced. 'Charlie, I can't ask you to...'

'It's OK. I have good memories of my engagement to Jess,' he said. 'We need these shots for the farm. I can do it if you can.'

She took the box from the sandcastle and handed it to him. He took the ring from the box and slid it onto the ring finger of her left hand, letting her snap a picture as he did so. The second photograph was of his right hand palm-up while her left hand was curled round it, showing off the ring with the sea and the blue sky in the background; and finally they stood with the sea behind them, her right arm wrapped around him and her left hand held out to display the ring, while he took the snap on her phone.

In another life, this could've been real.

And it was oh, so tempting.

But there was too much in the way.

'That should do,' she said. 'I don't know about you, but all that sandcastle-building has made me hungry. I vote we go and get some chips for lunch.'

'Works for me,' he said.

They headed for the pathway back to the town,

brushed the sand off their feet and slid their shoes back on, then walked along the raised path with its spectacular views across the marshes. She didn't have a clue what to say, so she used the excuse of concentrating on the scenery and taking more photographs; and Charlie didn't seem to be disposed to make conversation, either.

At the harbour front, she bought them both a box of chips; after liberal use of salt and vinegar, they sat and ate their chips on the harbour wall, closely watched by the seagulls.

'These are good,' Charlie said.

'Very,' she replied.

She was careful to keep smiling, but inside she was full of questions she couldn't answer.

Had she done the wrong thing, telling Charlie they should stick to being friends? Should she have taken a risk? But what if she took the risk and it went wrong?

As if he knew that she needed space, he didn't chatter on the way back to the car, and just put music on the stereo during the drive back to the farm.

She busied herself revising the farm website and added the photos to the farm's social media; and then, to distract herself and clear her head, she went for a walk. But, as she drew closer to the farmhouse after her walk, her phone started to chime with notifications.

Quickly, she checked them, worrying that something night have happened to one of her parents while her phone was out of range.

Her relief at not seeing a message from either of them was short-lived, because the rest of the messages made no sense.

Congratulations!

About time someone swept you off your feet!

And then the kicker, a private message from her boss.

When I asked you to take the campaign viral, I wasn't expecting you to get *engaged* to do it…

Engaged?

Then her knees turned to water as she realised just what a huge mistake she'd made. Instead of posting the photos to the farm's social media, she'd accidentally posted them on her own.

With the hashtags *#soromantic #dayattheseaside #beautifulnorfolk*, she'd posted a picture of the sandcastle with her grandmother's engagement ring, the one of Charlie slipping the ring onto her finger, and the two of them standing by the sea, showing off the ring.

Oh, no.

This was a disaster.

She was always so meticulous. How had she managed to make such a stupid, elementary error

Quickly, she logged into her account, deleted the posts and put them where they were supposed to be, on the farm's account: but it was too late. The messages still kept coming in. People she knew had reposted it onto their account, and people they knew had reposted it, and on and on it went...

She sent a quick message back to her boss.

Sea air clearly went to my head—posted shots to wrong account. It's for the farm. We're acting as models to save budget!

She sent the same message to her closest friends, though none of them seemed to believe her. They all wanted to know how and why she'd kept such a gorgeous man under wraps.

And then there was Charlie himself. She really needed to warn him about her mistake. He'd told her about his sister thinking they were dating; this went way, way beyond that.

She sent him a message.

Are you free? Need to talk to you pretty urgently about a tricky situation.

His reply was almost instantaneous.

Come over now.

When the knock came at his kitchen door, Charlie opened it and handed Elle a glass of wine before she'd even crossed the threshold.

'Thank you, but I think you might want to

throw this over me when you find out what I've done,' she said. 'I'm so sorry. Somehow I managed to post the pictures to my own social media instead of the farm's. Everyone I know thinks we're engaged, even though I've told them we're being models for the farm and it's all fake. And it's gone viral.'

'I kind of already know,' he said. 'Jo follows you on social media. She already asked me why I was keeping you a secret.'

'Oh.' Elle grimaced. 'I'll send her a direct message and apologise. I've put a note up about how all this lovely fresh air has turned me into an airhead who posted the wrong photos to the wrong account—my "fiancé" is actually my colleague and we're showcasing the farm, how it's the perfect place to get engaged and then married.' She shook her head. 'I'm so sorry I've been so ditsy. I don't have a clue how it happened. I never usually make this sort of stupid mistake.'

'Don't worry about it,' he said. Though he couldn't help wondering: what would it be like to be with her for real? Instead, he said, 'Actually, it's quite nice to know you're capable of making a mistake. It was beginning to be a bit scary, how perfect you are.'

'Perfect?' She scoffed. 'I'm just me.'

'You're not "just" anything, Elle Newton,' he said.

'Thank you.' Her eyes were wide and earnest. 'Though I wasn't fishing for compliments.'

'I know you weren't.'

She sighed. 'So what do we do now, Mr Fake Fiancé?'

'Carry on with the soft launch, Ms Fake Fiancée,' he said. 'How long until the shopping side is sorted?'

'Not long. Frieda's given me the artwork files I need, so I'm going to sort out the produce labels for the next lot of stock, as well as sorting the website header and making sure it's consistent across all the social media sites.'

'Good.' He paused. 'We might have something else that could go viral this week.'

'What?'

'Mulberry's due to calve any day now.'

'Ohh—you mean we could have a video of a calf taking its first wobbly steps?'

'Yup.'

'I'm in. Even if she goes into labour at ridiculous o'clock in the morning, call me,' she said.

'I will,' he promised. 'I love what you've done with the website so far. The way you've brought in interest. The videos of our bees in the wildflower meadow, and the dawn chorus, and the cows playing football, the lambs skipping about, and that owl swooping just above your head.'

'That last one was more luck than judgement,' she warned.

'But it works. If I didn't live here, I'd want to visit. I'd want to see the lambs waggling their tails like little helicopters, and the calves in your "moo-rning from Bluebell Farm" posts. I can't believe how many people log on to say "moo-rning" back.'

'They've all gone viral,' she said. 'People we don't know are copying and reposting. My boss is really pleased.'

'I'd want to come and try making cheese, have a go at spinning wool, and watch the deer foraging in the fields at dusk. I'd want to try the cake of the week in the café, and use your reference guide to name the flowers and the butterflies I see on my visit, and watch the swans at the pond, and see the damselflies flitting about. What you've done to the website makes this feel a really exciting, happening place.'

'It *is* an exciting, happening place,' she said.

He didn't push her on it, but he was secretly pleased. At last she'd moved past her bad memories of West Byfield and could see the farm for what it was.

'Give it a couple of weeks for the schedule to

be firmed up, and all the new sessions the café team suggested will be in place,' she said. 'The toddler group, the knit-and-natter sessions, the silver surfer group, and the coffee-and-crafting club. I think you might need to recruit some extra staff in a couple of months, even if it's for mid-morning to mid-afternoon shifts.'

'Not just that,' he said. 'Our accommodation's fully booked for the summer, and we have a waiting list for that and the courses. And I've had a couple of enquiries about weddings, despite the fact we did it as a soft launch. I've got people wanting to know how big the barn is and if we'll have a wedding fair here.'

'Cake-bakers, florists, dressmakers, balloon suppliers, and the like,' she said. 'It's a really good idea. Hold a wedding fair once every six months. That way you'll get the spring and summer brides at one, and the autumn and winter brides at the other.' She smiled. 'So, despite the mess I made of posting the pictures today, you're happy with the job I'm doing?'

'More than happy,' he said.

'Good.' She finished her glass of wine. 'I think Rav is going to wait for me to come back to London before we have the official chat, but he did say he was pleased with the way this job is going.'

'So you'll get your promotion?'

'Let's just say that next week I think I'll be ticking off the next step in my five-year plan,' she said.

'Congratulations. I'm really pleased for you,' he said.

Though part of him didn't want Elle to leave. He loved working alongside her, and he'd felt more happy and fulfilled than he had for years. He loved being with her.

And he had a horrible idea that it was more than that: was he developing feelings for her? Or was it even more than that? Was he falling in love with her? With the bright, sparkly, confident woman who was full of ideas and saw the joy in things. With the woman who was facing up to her past, owning the misery she'd felt and was moving past it. She didn't have that slightly pinched look in her eyes any more, at the farm. She fitted right in to the community. She was fast becoming the heart of the farm, for him.

But he knew she wanted to go back to London, and he wanted to stay here. There was no middle ground. So, much as he wanted to ask her to move their friendship into a real relationship, he wasn't going to put that pressure on her. He'd let her go, unburdened by guilt at leaving him behind. They'd stay friends.

And he hoped that in London she'd find someone who deserved her: someone who could give her what he couldn't.

CHAPTER EIGHT

ON MONDAY AFTERNOON, Charlie noticed that Mulberry was in the early stages of calving: she was restless, off her food, and there was a dip between the head of her tail and the pin-bones. Her tummy seemed less full, because the calf was moving into the birth canal, and she'd separated herself from the rest of the herd.

He disinfected the calving pen and added plenty of clean bedding, then brought her in to the pen. Then he messaged Elle.

Mulberry likely to calve today. Will keep you posted.

Do you know when?

No. Checking every three hours. She's in the calving pen in the barn.

And at one o'clock in the morning, he knew Mulberry was in labour. He had everything prepared in case she needed him to help her; now it was a waiting game.

One in the morning really wasn't a good time

to call someone; but on the other hand Elle had been adamant that she wanted him to let her know, even at ridiculous o'clock.

She answered on the third ring. 'Is Mulberry having her calf?'

'Yes. I'm in the barn with her, if you want to come and join us.'

'On my way,' she said.

She turned up a few minutes later, in jeans and a sweater, which he suspected she might've pulled on over her pyjamas, and wellies. 'I haven't seen a calf born in years. Is this her first one?'

'Yes. I've got gloves and lubricant and equipment in case she needs help.' He looked at her. 'So you know the routine?'

'For an uncomplicated birth, yes. Though I don't remember enough to be much use other than calling the vet for you.' She handed him a travel mug. 'Coffee.'

'Thank you.'

They sat on a bale of straw, giving Mulberry space. The cow was lying down, now, and starting to strain and push.

'I can see two feet,' she said. 'Front feet, so the calf is head-first.'

'Normal presentation. That's good,' he said. He pulled his gloves on. 'As soon as the head's out, I'll give her a little help. I had a good tip from your dad: cross the front legs of the calf and turn it so its backbone is eleven o'clock to its mum's backbone. That prevents the calf's hips getting stuck and saves the mum from a pinched nerve.'

He did exactly as he'd said to her, and the birth was fast after that, with the calf slithering out. He gave Mulberry a drink of lukewarm water, and helped her to her feet.

Mulberry sniffed her calf, her tail swishing, and started to lick the calf.

Elle took a couple of shots, her phone on silent so there wouldn't be any noise to disturb the cow and her new calf. 'I'd forgotten how amazing it is to see a newborn. She's licking the calf to stimulate blood flow and muscle movement, isn't she?'

'And to help it dry off from the amniotic fluid. She'll deliver the placenta in the next three hours and the calf should stand in the next half an hour,' he said.

He checked the calf, then came back to join Elle on the straw bale. 'We have a girl. She looks normal and healthy. I'll give her a temporary neck band to ID her, but I'll fit her ear tag tomorrow.'

This was really special, Elle thought: just Charlie, herself, the cow and her newborn calf in the dimly lit barn. The first moments of new life, in the middle of the night; they didn't need to talk because this was just perfect.

A few minutes later, the calf got to her feet, all wobbly, and Elle took pictures of the calf's first few steps.

'She's gorgeous,' Elle whispered, looking at the pure white calf with her perfect black ears and nose. 'I've never seen such long eyelashes.'

'Yeah, she's a beauty,' Charlie agreed.

Mulberry lowed gently to encourage her calf to stand; she was answered by a high-pitched moo from the calf. Mulberry stood still, letting the calf work out what to do, and finally the calf nuzzled her mum and began to suck, her tail swishing.

'This is amazing,' Elle said softly, taking Charlie's hand and squeezing it briefly. 'Such a privilege.'

'Do you want to name her?' he asked.

'Can I?'

He smiled. 'If you can think up a berry name we haven't used yet.'

'The current calves are Bilberry, Cranberry and Loganberry, right?' she asked.

'Yes.'

She thought about it. 'How about Huckleberry?'

'Huckleberry works for me,' he said, and sang a snatch of 'Moon River'.

She smiled as they leaned on the gate, watching Huckleberry and Mulberry together.

'Let's give them a bit of bonding time,' he said quietly.

She turned to face him, and the next thing she knew he'd pulled her into his arms. Hers wrapped around him, and they were kissing.

Her blood felt as if it was sizzling. She'd never wanted anyone so much in her life.

He broke the kiss and leaned his forehead against hers. 'I know we said we were going to stick to being just friends and colleagues,' he whispered, 'but I want you so badly, Elle. You make me ache. I dream of you. You're in my head, all the time. I can't think straight, any more.'

'Same here,' she whispered back. 'I know it can't be forever, because we want different things, but maybe just for a little while? I think I'd regret it otherwise.' He nodded, as if agreeing that this couldn't last, but they had right now. 'Take me to bed, Charlie.'

'Sure?'

'Very sure,' she said.

It took them a while to get back to his cottage, because they kept having to stop and kiss.

By the time they got there, every nerve end felt as if it was fizzing. He looked just as hot and bothered as she felt.

Both of them kicked off their wellies, and it took him three seconds to strip off his boiler suit. Underneath he was wearing a pair of jeans and nothing else. She sucked in a breath. 'Do you have any idea how hot you look, right now?' An environmental warrior, his muscles toned from hard work and his skin tanned by the sun.

His answer was to kiss her, scoop her up and carry her to his room.

She had no idea which of them took off the other's clothes; she was too swept away with that visceral need for him.

Then, just when he'd laid her back against the pillows, he paused.

Adrenaline fluttered through her. Had he changed his mind? Was he thinking about Jess? 'What's wrong?' she asked, inwardly dreading the answer.

He grimaced, and she braced herself for the worst.

'I hate to tell you this, but I don't have any condoms,' he said.

She almost laughed with relief. He wasn't rejecting her; he was being sensible. 'Neither do I,' she said. 'But I don't want to stop, because right now I want you so much I think I'm going to spontaneously combust.'

'Me, too—but we need to be sensible,' he said.

'We will be.' She kept her gaze firmly fixed on his, and loved the way his eyes darkened when she said, 'Because there are other things we can do that *don't* need a condom.' His eyes darkened further when she moistened her lower lip with the tip of her tongue.

'Oh, God, yes,' he said, and his voice was so raspy and sexy that she went hot all over.

She held out her arms and he kissed her again; and then he kissed his way down her body, exploring her with his hands and his mouth until all she could see were fireworks inside her head. She exchanged touch for touch, kiss for kiss, exploring him in turn and delighting in discovering what made him gasp and what made his body surge. And then, finally, when she'd come apart in his arms, he drew the covers over them, holding her close. Cherishing her.

When she woke, a couple of hours later, Charlie was gone. Assuming he'd gone to check on Mulberry and her new calf, she dressed and headed down to his kitchen. His wellies were gone, so she knew her guess had been right; she made coffee, and took two mugs out to the barn.

Charlie was sitting on the bale of straw next to the pen, and looked up as she walked in. 'Hey. Sorry to desert you. I was just checking on our girls.'

'That's what I assumed,' she said, handing him a mug. 'How are they?'

'Mulberry's fine. She's delivered the after-birth and I'm happy she's doing well. I'll do all the registration stuff with your dad later. And thank you for the coffee.'

'Pleasure. How's Huckleberry doing?'

'She's doing great. They're both having a rest on the straw right now.' He glanced at his watch. 'The sun will be up in half an hour. The sky's at its prettiest right now, so it might be a good shot for your blog.'

The last sunrise she'd photographed, he'd put his arms around her to keep her from shivering. This time, his arms were round her because he wanted her close. Just as she wanted him close. And how good it made her feel.

The birds sang their heads off to greet the new day, and the sun rose over the treeline, a big burnt-orange ball in a pale peach sky.

'Hear the skylark?' he asked.

She looked up, trying to see the bird that had soared up to sing in the dawn, the song going on for so much longer than that of the robins and blackbirds: but all she could see was sky, even as she heard the song.

'"And drowned in yonder living blue/The lark becomes a sightless song",' she quoted.

'Is that Shelley?' he asked.

She shook her head. 'Tennyson, *In Memoriam*. Shelley's *To a Skylark* starts "Hail to thee, blithe Spirit!"'

'I'm going to have a lot of reading to do, to keep up with you,' he teased.

'I'll make you a reading list,' she teased back. 'Poetry for farmers.'

'Moo-etry,' he said, riffing on the way the local dialect pronounced 'oh' as 'oo'.

Just like the way the bullies of her teens had changed Newton to Moo-ton. Except that memory didn't hurt any more. Charlie had given her a different perspective on the past. She'd always be grateful to him for that.

Except the farm *was* her past, wasn't it? Her life was in London, now. And she'd be going back to it soon. Leaving him behind.

The problem was, last night had made her feel differently. Raised all sort of questions. Ones she didn't want to tackle right now, when she was still half-asleep; she needed to think about it properly. This was something that needed handling carefully, when her brain was sharp.

Eventually he said, 'Nice as it is, sitting here with you, I'd better get on with the milking, or the cows are going to be so grumpy with me.'

Before she could offer to help, he added, 'And you had a broken night with Huckleberry. Go and get some sleep.'

Huckleberry wasn't the only reason she'd had a broken night.

And right then she felt completely confused about the situation.

Maybe he was right. She needed sleep.

'I'll catch you later,' she said lightly, and headed back to the farmhouse. Her father was in the kitchen, making a pot of tea.

'Mulberry had her calf last night,' she said.

'Charlie texted me. You called her Huckleberry. Good name,' Mike said approvingly. 'It's a magical moment, watching those first wobbly steps, isn't it?'

'Amazing,' she said. 'I took some film. I'm going to put it up on the farm's website today.'

'Get some sleep, first, love. You must be shattered,' he said, patting her shoulder.

Elle gave in and went to bed, but every time she closed her eyes she thought of Charlie. The way he'd touched her, the way he'd made her feel...

She wanted him and she wanted to be with him, but her whole life was in London. Everything she'd worked for. If she gave it all up, it was a huge risk. She'd never managed to pick Mr Right. Would she be setting herself up for heartache all over again?

Falling for her fake fiancé would be the most stupid thing she could do.

Except she had a nasty feeling she'd already done it.

CHAPTER NINE

A POWER NAP HELPED; and then Elle did what she always did when things were going wrong in her personal life. She threw herself into work.

This particular part of the project felt a bit too close to the bone, now, but she'd pretend it was all for someone else. Which it *was*, really: she was showcasing the romantic side of the farm to tempt their future brides and grooms. It wasn't real. She needed to remind herself that it wasn't going to become real, either, and keep her head straight.

Charlie Webb was her parents' business partner and her friend. Nothing more, nothing less.

And she'd be leaving Bluebell Farm at the end of the week.

She sent him a quick text.

Setting up the wedding barn. Still OK to act as groom tomorrow afternoon? Thanks, E

No kiss.

Because this was business.

So it was ridiculous to feel hurt when the reply came back, OK. Let me know timings. C

Also no kiss.

Was that because he, too, saw this as a business communication? Or had he had the space to think about it, and come to the same conclusion that she had: that they'd made a huge mistake in sleeping together?

'Think of Mum and Dad,' she told herself fiercely. 'The farm needs to be a success.' Because, if it wasn't and her parents ran out of money—including Charlie's investment—they'd be forced to sell. Meaning that not only would they lose their dream, they'd lose generations of family history.

So, much as the fake fiancée/wedding business rattled her, she'd simply have to put up with it. For their sakes.

A couple of calls netted her most of the window dressing she needed; she could pick everything up later today, do the shoot with Frieda tomorrow afternoon, and finalise the website details in the evening. She'd take Thursday to wrap things up, and Friday she could be on the train to London.

Back to her proper life.

But first she needed to talk some of it over with her mum and Lisa in the farm shop café.

'So you're planning a fake wedding?' Lisa asked.

'We're doing a mock-up of a wedding venue for publicity photos,' Elle corrected. 'Until we've actually hosted a wedding and the bride and groom have agreed to let us use photos for publicity, we can't show people what sort of thing they can expect. The barn's an amazing space, but potential clients need to see it as it could be.' Elle spread her hands. 'So we're going to photograph the barn set up as a wedding venue. Well, not me—Frieda is. She's a landscape specialist, but she's agreed to take the publicity photos for us.'

'So what are you thinking?' Angie asked.

'We need to show the ceremony area, the wedding breakfast area, and the dance area.' Elle ticked them off on her fingers. 'I've talked to the willow weaving people, and they're going to lend us an arch and a few big willow heart outlines that we can decorate with fairy lights, gauzy fabric and flowers. We can set up an aisle with, say, twenty-four chairs, to give the feel of a small family wedding. And we'll set up a couple of tables with cutlery, glasses, table confetti and flowers. That leaves the dance floor area; I'm hiring some of those big light-up letters to spell out "love", and we'll have the hearts on the wall.'

'What about a cake?' Angie asked. 'You can't have a wedding without a cake.'

'I could go into town and pick up a couple of those ready-iced plain wedding cakes, and we'll add wild flowers or something to dress it up,' Elle said.

'No. We're about doing things locally. I'll make the cake,' Lisa said.

'But you don't have enough time to ice it,' Elle said.

'I don't need to. Naked cakes are trendy,' Lisa said. 'That's what my niece had at her wedding.' She flicked into her phone and showed Elle the photograph. 'It's not formally iced all the way round—it's decorated with a bit of chocolate drip, and then flowers and berries.'

'That'd be brilliant,' Elle said. 'Could you do something like that, ready for tomorrow afternoon?'

'Definitely,' Lisa said. 'And then we can give away free slices in the café—I don't think it's fair to sell it, when we've used it for a prop.'

'And it's also good publicity,' Elle said. 'I can print up some cards to go with them, directing people to the website, and tell them to pass it on to anyone in their family and friends who might be thinking about weddings.'

'We can dress all the chairs for the ceremony with ivory sashes, and maybe have petals and tea-lights on the borders of the aisle,' Angie suggested.

'That'd be wonderful,' Elle said.

'What about the bride and groom?' Angie asked. 'Who are you getting to do that? Models from London?'

'No. We don't have the budget.' Elle took a deep breath. 'Charlie and I are doing it.'

Angie's eyes widened. 'Are you sure? I mean...'

'I asked him last week—and, yes, I was sensitive about how I phrased it—and he agreed,' Elle said.

'What about your dress, Elle?' Angie asked.

'Already sorted,' Elle reassured her. 'I bought it in a charity shop in Norwich last week. There's a short veil and a flower crown, too. Charlie can wear his sharp London suit.'

'Flowers?' Lisa asked.

'I'm keeping it simple.' She smiled. 'The obvious thing would be a posy of bluebells.'

'Scarlett in the shop is really good with displays,' Lisa said. 'She's really creative. And she did the flowers for my niece's wedding. We could ask her to do the flowers.'

'And any other ideas for styling the barn or the tables,' Elle said. 'Can we bring her in now?'

'I'll go and get her,' Lisa said.

When she'd gone, Angie turned to Elle. 'Sitting here, planning a wedding reception with you—I wish we were doing this for real.'

Elle felt the colour sweep into her face. 'I'm sorry. I wanted you involved because the farm's yours. It didn't occur to me that you might…' She blew out a breath. 'I never meant to hurt you, Mum. But I have to be honest with you. I just don't think I'll ever find Mr Right.'

She ignored how she'd felt when Charlie had kissed her. When he'd swept her off her feet and up to his bed. There was too much in the way for it to work between them.

'I don't mean to pressure you, love,' Angie said.

'I know. Love you, Mum.'

'Love you, too.' Angie hugged her. 'And you know your dad and I are so proud of you, don't you?'

Elle's throat was too thick with unshed tears for her to reply. She simply nodded.

Scarlett turned out to be full of great ideas, and between them they came up with the perfect wedding day. Elle spent the rest of the day picking up props, but she had a case of severely cold feet by the end of the day.

How could she get this to work, when there was still unfinished business between her and Charlie? Any awkwardness between them would show in the photographs, and undercut what they were trying to do. She needed to make sure they were on the same page.

She texted him.

Can we talk?

It was a while before he replied, with a cagey When?

Whenever's convenient.

She hoped he'd pick up that she meant as soon as possible.

He typed back.

Free now.

Thanks. Coming over.

But she didn't want to sit in his kitchen and remember the last time she'd been in his cottage.

Maybe we can go for a walk?

Works for me.

So he didn't want to sit in his kitchen with her either. She wasn't sure whether that was a good thing or not.

Where would they go? Not the bluebell woods, she decided: she'd spend all the time there thinking of that kiss. And the kiss on the beach. And the kiss near newborn Huckleberry. Near the shepherd's huts was also a bad idea, because then she'd think about dancing with him.

'Thanks for making time,' she said when he answered the door. 'I thought we could walk by the wildflower meadow.'

'Good idea,' he said.

She didn't try making small talk. And he waited until they'd reached the wildflower meadows before asking, 'So what did you want to talk about?'

'The shoot tomorrow,' she said. 'If it's awkward between us, it'll show. And then the pictures won't be any use.'

'So we have to discuss the elephant in the room. Not that we're in a room.' He shrugged. 'All right. You go first.'

'I…' Where did she start? 'For the record, I don't just hop into bed with anyone.'

He frowned. 'Of course you don't. I never for a minute thought you were like that.'

'Good.' She huffed out a breath. Why was this so difficult? 'Charlie—I like you. In other circumstances…' But it wasn't going to work, was it? 'Since I've been here, you've made me see that the farm isn't the awful place I built it

up to be in my head and I can enjoy it again.
I'm grateful that you've shown me I can come
back and it's fine. People aren't going to make
me feel like an outsider. They don't see me as—
well, how I was as a teen.'

'But?'

Either it showed on her face, or he was really
perceptive. 'My life's in London,' she said simply. 'My five-year plan's there. I've worked hard
for that promotion. I'd intended to go back to a
job I really, really want.' She paused. This was
where she had to be brave. 'But then there's you.
And you're here.' She couldn't read his expression. At all. But if they didn't get this out in the
open, it was going to simmer away until it ex-
ploded in their faces. 'OK. Cards on table. I'm
terrified of saying this. I have no idea what's in
your head, and if I say what's in mine there's a
chance that it's going to make things even more
complicated. And we need that photo shoot tomorrow to be perfect.' She took a deep breath.
'But if I don't say it…things are going to be
complicated anyway.'

His eyes narrowed. 'You're the communications expert, Elle. Right now I have no idea
where this is going.'

'I'll keep it simple. I'm going back to London
on Friday.' The words were stuck in her throat.
This could be a disaster. If he said no, this time

she'd know that she'd been rejected for who she was, not where she came from. If he said yes, then it might be fabulous at first: but what if he started to resent her for wrecking his own five-year plan? She closed her eyes to stop the words spinning. 'Will you come back to London with me?'

'Come back to London with you,' he repeated.

She couldn't tell a thing from the tone of his voice. But if she opened her eyes and looked at him, she knew she wouldn't have the courage to say the rest of it. 'I know you hate London. I know it's where Jess died. But you taught me that I could move on and love Bluebell Farm again. Maybe I can teach you to move on and love London again. I don't mean forget Jess, I mean be in a place where you can cherish her memory and let yourself love again.'

Elle was a lot braver than he was, Charlie thought. He'd been thinking about this ever since they'd slept together; even though they'd agreed that it was just a one-off, a moment out of time, it had thrown him into a spin. He liked her—more than liked her—but there was so much in the way.

Yeah. She was right. It was complicated.

With Elle by his side, he thought he could finally move on.

Although he didn't want to go back to his

old job, he still had a good network and he was pretty sure he'd be able to find something working with environmentally friendly funds.

But.

Bluebell Farm had changed him.

His heart belonged here, now. He didn't want to go back to London.

'Maybe we can work things out between us,' he said, 'but not in London. I'll be honest with you, too. Looking back, I don't like the person I was, when I lived in London. I've changed, and I don't want to be that person again.'

'So what you're saying is that you'd be with me—but only if I stayed here?' she asked. 'How could that work? Commuting would be terrible: half an hour from here to Norwich, two hours on the train, half an hour on the Tube, and then three hours at the other end of the day. With that sort of travel time factored in, we'd barely see each other.'

'What about working in London during the week and spending your weekends here?' he suggested. 'That way, we'd both get what we wanted.'

She looked thoughtful, then shook her head. 'I'd be trying to split myself between the two parts of my life, and I'd feel that I wasn't giving enough to either of them.'

She didn't want to stay here; so, if he wanted

to be with her, he'd have to be the one to move. Go back to London. Back to the daily drag of commuting. Back to working ridiculous hours in a culture that expected him to be seen in the office every possible minute. Back to not being able to breathe. 'I just can't do London,' he said softly. 'Even for you. I'm sorry. I could try, but I already know I'd feel trapped and smothered— even if I had a part-time job in the City and we had an allotment and a huge garden so I could spend half the week outdoors. I'd end up resenting you for making me go back. And if you stayed here for me, you'd end up resenting me because you'd lose all the opportunities you have in London.'

Elle knew he was right. She wouldn't be able to change his mind about London.

But if she stayed here for him... What if he changed his mind about her, too? Then she'd be left with nothing. The risk was terrifying and even the thought of it sent ice slithering through her veins.

She'd secretly hoped that Charlie might be falling for her, the way she'd found herself falling for him; but clearly he wasn't. Or, at least, not enough. Although her feelings about the farm had changed, and she'd found a man who also loved it and didn't think less of her for her background… At the moment, it was hypothetical and they were both assuming he could make space in his life for her. But she knew that losing Jess had hit him hard. If Elle wasn't enough for him to go to London, then who was to say she'd be enough for him here? Pining for him in London when she didn't have to see him was one thing; staying here and seeing him every day, getting more and more miserable, would be even worse.

'There isn't a viable compromise, is there?' she asked.

'I can't see one.' He drew in a breath. 'I'm sorry. You're the one woman I would try it for.'

'But you already know you'd be unhappy.' Because she wasn't enough for him.

'Just as you'd be unhappy here.' He paused. 'As you said, in other circumstances it could've been wonderful between us. But I can't see a compromise that would work for both of us. I don't want you to leave; but I also don't want you to stay here and be unhappy. It's not fair to ask you to give up everything for me.'

She reached out and touched his face. 'I wish things were different. That we could be together in London. But you're right. I don't want you to be here, miles away from me; but I don't want you to be unhappy in London, either.'

'Bottom line: to be fair to both of us, all I can offer you is friendship, Elle,' he said.

Just as he had, the very first time she'd met him and he'd let her sob out her misery onto his shoulder.

'Friends it is,' she said, smiling widely despite the fact that she wanted to curl into a ball and sob her heart out. 'So we're OK for the photo shoot tomorrow?'

'Yeah. We're OK,' he said.

'Great. I have stuff to do,' she said, striving for brightness and breeziness. 'I'll see you tomorrow.'

Wednesday. The wedding day.

Well, the not-wedding day. The acting wedding day. The day when they were mocking up the barn as if there was a wedding, but the wedding wasn't happening.

Weirdly, Charlie found himself as nervous as if it was real. As if his best man was running through the checklist to make sure they hadn't forgotten anything; as if his mum was checking that his buttonhole looked right and his tie was straight; as if his sister was all thrilled that her eighteen-month-old daughter Ivy was going to toddle down the aisle behind Elle as a flower girl.

None of it was happening.

It was just photographs.

He hadn't even been involved in dressing the barn; he'd offered to help, but Elle had sent him a very polite text saying that it was quite all right, thank you, because she, her mum, Lisa and Scarlett had everything under control. All he had to do was turn up for a couple of photographs at three o'clock.

He arrived at five minutes to three, knowing that Elle would be a stickler for time.

And the transformation of the barn was amazing.

She'd said something about borrowing a willow arch; there it was, by a small table, covered in gauzy ivory fabric, greenery and fairy lights.

The limewashed chiavari chairs were set out in two sections with an aisle in between, as if ready for an intimate family wedding, the backs dressed with simple ivory sashes. There were ivory flower petals marking the edges of the aisle, and tiny globe vases filled with more fairy lights.

The centre of the barn was set up for the wedding breakfast: two round tables, with damask tablecloths. The cutlery was gleaming, as were the glasses; there was an ivory enamelled jug in the centre of each table, filled with a delicate spray of wild flowers. Each place was set with a small ivory box, which he assumed were empty and represented the wedding favours; each was tied with a narrow gold ribbon to match the gold hearts of the table confetti, and a single stem of bluebells adorned the boxes.

There was a small table set with a cake; instead of being covered in icing, it was decorated with flowers and berries, and the word 'love' in a fancy script as a cake topper.

At the dance floor end, there were enormous letters made of lights, spelling out the word 'love'; on the walls there were willow hearts, festooned with the same greenery, gauzy fabric and fairy lights as the bridal arch.

'This is stunning,' he said as Angie came over to him. 'It really looks like…' He dragged in a breath. 'Just wow. You've all worked so hard.'

But where was Elle?

He knew she wasn't there, because even if his back had been turned he would've known where she was. He would've felt her presence.

Hoping he sounded a lot more casual than he felt, he enquired, 'Where's Elle?'

'Gone to change,' Angie said. 'So you like what we've done?'

'It's amazing,' he said.

'A lot of the ideas were Elle's and Scarlett's,' Lisa said, coming over to join them. 'I think we might have our wedding co-ordinator role covered.'

Elle? Or Scarlett?

'It's perfect,' he said. 'And I really like that cake.'

'My idea,' Lisa said, and turned slightly pink. 'Though it's not just a prop. We're giving out free slices in the café, afterwards, with a card telling people about the wedding services.'

'It's great,' he said.

'Ah, here's our bride,' Frieda, the photographer, called.

He turned, almost as if he really were waiting for Elle at the altar. She was wearing a simple ivory strapless dress with a beaded bodice, a short veil attached to her hair with a narrow crown of ivory flowers, and she was carrying a sheaf of bluebells.

Was this the wedding of her dreams—the wedding she thought she'd never have?

Charlie couldn't say a word. His tongue was definitely stuck to the roof of his mouth. With superglue.

Every step she took towards him made him ache a little bit more.

He wanted her. Wanted to be with her. Wanted to make his life with her.

But he just couldn't do it in London. Not any more.

'Hi,' she said quietly as she reached him. 'What do you think?'

She was talking about the barn. 'Stunning.' He was talking about her.

'I'd recommend Scarlett as your wedding co-ordinator. She has great ideas.'

He nodded. 'Lisa said.'

'Shall we?'

He'd never seen himself as an actor, but now he would have to act his socks off.

Or maybe he wouldn't. Maybe he just had to imagine that this was real, that Elle had walked down the aisle towards him. That they'd found a workable compromise and today was the first day of the rest of their lives.

So he smiled.

Even when Angie and Lisa set off a dried petal confetti cannon, and Frieda took shot after shot of himself and Elle.

Even when they posed to cut the cake.

Even when Angie, a huge Bryan Adams fan, whipped out her phone and started playing '(Everything I Do) I Do It For You' while he and Elle danced with the letters as a background and Frieda snapped away.

'And that's a wrap,' Frieda said at last. 'I'm going to do a bit of post production at home, Elle, but I'll send you the link to the private files in a couple of hours.'

'That's fabulous, Frieda. Thank you.' Elle stepped away from him. 'Thank you, team.

We've done a great job. I'll help clear up, then I'm going back to the farmhouse to finish off putting most of this together, so all I have to do is slot Frieda's photos in.'

'Go now. I'll do the clearing up,' Charlie said, 'because I didn't do anything to help, this morning.'

'Are you sure?' Angie asked.

'I'm sure,' Charlie said.

'I'll save you a slice of cake,' Lisa promised, and patted his shoulder.

It didn't take long to put the cutlery and glasses back in their boxes, fold the tablecloth and the sashes back into their boxes, and sweep up the confetti and stack the chairs and tables.

Charlie was glad he had the afternoon milking to take his mind off things.

And when Elle texted him later, to ask if he wanted to be involved in choosing the photos, he texted back,

That's OK, trust your judgement.

So he wasn't even going to come and help choose the photographs?

Elle stifled the hurt, telling herself to be reasonable about it. It wasn't so surprising, was it? Today must've brought back a million memories of his real wedding—and his loss.

She texted back.

If you want to take a look, here's the link.

And then she got on with choosing the photos with her parents.

Frieda had done a fantastic job. But Elle just hoped that nobody noticed the expression on her face and guessed what she really felt about Charlie Webb, her fake fiancé and her fake bridegroom.

Ten minutes after she'd loaded the last bit of the website, her phone pinged.

Charlie?

Of course not. She damped down the disappointment and opened her boss's note.

Website fabulous. Looking forward to toasting our new senior account manager with champagne on Monday. Congratulations, Elle!

'Was that Charlie?' Mike asked.

'No. My boss. I got the promotion,' she said, and the tears spilled over. She just hoped her parents thought they were tears of joy rather than tears that she was walking away from Charlie. 'So I'll be going back to London for definite on Friday.'

'Elle.' Angie wrapped her arms round her daughter. 'I'll miss you so much. Are you sure you won't stay? You couldn't work remotely for the agency from here?'

'No,' Elle said, as gently as she could. 'But I'll be back soon, Mum.'

'You can't stay until Sunday?' Mike asked.

'I've got tons to do in London before Monday,' she said. 'But it doesn't mean I don't love you. And I promise I will definitely visit more.'

'Then we'll drive you to the station,' Mike said.

Her dad's pick-up might be jolty and a far cry from the comfort of Charlie's Range Rover, but at least she wouldn't have to face Charlie again. Face all the loss.

'Thanks, Dad. I'd better start packing. Love you,' she said.

CHAPTER TEN

GOING BACK TO London on Friday morning was harder than she'd expected. Saying goodbye to the animals was hard. She was almost in tears as she hugged the calves. She made a fuss of the sheep, and gave the hens some mealworms that had them thanking her very vocally and Carbon the rooster doing a dance. She had a last walk by the wildflower meadow and in the woods to say goodbye to the swans.

Last time she'd been here, she couldn't get away quickly enough.

This time—leaving was much harder.

The news had spread quickly, and Elle was shocked by how many visitors she had on Thursday. Rosie, with a pair of the softest gloves knitted from the wool of Bluebell Farm's sheep. Frieda, with a watercolour of the farm. Nicki, from the willow weavers, with a beautiful woven heart. Lisa, with a carrot cake. Scarlett, with a beautifully styled box full of goodies. 'It's from all the café and shop team,' she said, 'but it's also a prototype hamper.' She beamed. 'I'm thinking Christmas. And then we can offer seasonal variations.'

The only person who didn't come to see her was Charlie. She'd thought she might see him while she was saying goodbye to the animals, but he was clearly avoiding her. She'd texted him, to let him know that she started her new job on Monday and was going back to London on Friday, but his reply had been cool.

Congratulations. I'm pleased for you.

Well, that told her where she stood.

Right at the far edge of the friend zone. Where it was civil, not warm.

And it was only when Elle was on the train back to London on Friday morning that she realised how much she'd secretly been hoping that Charlie would drive to the station, sweep her off her feet before she could go through the barrier to the platform, and tell her that he was only letting her go temporarily and he was going to join her in London.

Friends.

That had been the deal.

So she'd go back to London. Back to her lovely, busy life. And she'd try not to miss him.

Though that was easier said than done. Despite meeting up with friends for lunch and drinks over the weekend to celebrate her new job, and getting back into the routine of gym classes, she found herself feeling lonely.

Everyone celebrated in the office when Rav officially announced her appointment as Senior Account Manager; she'd brought in cakes, fruit and bubbly, and Hugo took her and the senior management team out for an upmarket lunch. Everyone oohed and aahed over the lambs and the calves on the Bluebell Farm website, tried doing their own version of Carbon the rooster's special dance, and came up with terrible puns involving 'moo' that she wrote down for future use.

When a huge bouquet of flowers arrived for her at Reception, she looked at the name on the card and caught her breath.

Charlie.

Did this mean…?

Heart pounding, she read the message.

Congratulations on your promotion—very well deserved. Now go and shine. Best, Charlie

Anyone who didn't know what had happened between them would think this was simply a message from a grateful client. But she knew differently. This was Charlie making it clear that he was staying put and telling her to be happy in London. To shine.

Right.

Shine.

How, when she felt more like a rainy Wednesday afternoon than a Saturday lunchtime with blue skies and a blazing sun?

Flowers had been a good idea, Charlie thought. And that message. Elle would know what he was really saying, telling her to shine. That he wished he could be different, but he couldn't, so he wouldn't hold her back.

The problem was, he missed her.

He missed her helping out with the milking and singing to the cows.

He missed her gleefully telling him random facts she'd found about something on the farm.

He missed her straight talking and her teasing.

And the bed he'd always slept in alone, except for that half a night with her, felt huge and empty. Now, it was nothing more than a place to lay his head.

Without Elle, nothing felt right. Food tasted of nothing. Even the cows noticed, and nudged him and licked his face and lowed softly in his ear as if to tell him to cheer up, it might never happen.

Except it had, and it was his own fault. She'd

asked him to go to London with her. He'd said no. So he'd just have to fake it until life felt back on an even keel again.

'Earth to Elle?'

'Sorry, Marce. Busy day,' Elle said, smiling at her best friend.

Marcie coughed. 'Busy fortnight, more like. You haven't been the same since you've been back in London. And don't try to flannel me that it's because you're busy in your new role. The Elle Newton I know and love is the empress of project management. You're the epitome of the busy woman to ask if you want something done. You *thrive* on it. So what's really wrong?'

Elle bit her lip. 'You mean, who's Mr Wrong, this time?'

'No,' Marcie said. 'Because whenever you get let down by a bloke who was never good enough for you in the first place, you pick yourself up, dust yourself down, and go and find something fun to do. Right now,' she said gently, 'I don't think you're enjoying anything. Not your new job, not the film we saw last night—you were in another world, not paying any attention to it—not dinner out with the girls, and not cocktails the other night. So what's wrong, Elle? And what can I do to help you fix it?'

Elle sighed. 'This is in strictest confidence, right?'

'I'm your best friend. Of *course* it's in strictest confidence,' Marcie said, looking hurt.

'I know that. Sorry. I didn't mean to insult you. I'm all over the place.' Elle sighed again, and told her about Charlie. 'And there's no way of compromising,' she said. 'He doesn't want to be in London.'

'And you told him you don't want to be at Bluebell Farm,' Marcie said, giving her a hug. 'But, the way you've talked to me about the place, I'd say you've fallen back in love with it, as well as with him.'

'I have,' Elle admitted. 'But my job's here. There's no compromise.'

'Isn't there?' Marcie held up her forefinger. 'Firstly, there's this little thing called remote working—you could spend maybe one day a week in London and the rest in Norfolk. If the alternative's not having you at all, I reckon Rav's not going to refuse you.'

'Even with our spotty Wi-Fi?'

'If it's that desperate, go into town to send the emails and do the video calls,' Marcie said, and held up her middle finger to join the first. 'Secondly, you want to set up your own agency, eventually. Who says it can't be at the farm?'

Elle considered it. 'Why didn't Charlie or I think of that?' she asked.

'Because I think you were both too busy falling in love with each other and then panicking your socks off,' Marcie said.

'You're right,' Elle said with a sigh. 'We both panicked and weren't thinking straight.'

'What do you want, Elle?' Marcie asked.

'Everything. I want Charlie, I want to be part of everything that's happening at the farm, I want my parents, I want my friends, I want my job here, I want a Labrador puppy...' Her voice faded. 'But I can't have it all, can I?'

'Not all of the time, no,' Marcie said. 'But you can have all of it, some of the time. Be with the man you love, make your job more flexible, come and party once in a while in London, and invite us all down to cuddle the lambs and eat too much cake.'

'All of it, some of the time,' Elle repeated. Could she?

Marcie nodded. 'Honey, you need to talk to Charlie. Tell him what you told me. But face to face, not on the phone or even in a video call. He needs to look into your eyes so he knows what's in your heart.'

Elle glanced at her watch. 'If I leave in the next thirty minutes, I can get a train back to Norwich and a taxi to the farm. And if Charlie turns me down again…then I'll get the six o'clock train in to Liverpool Street tomorrow morning and just be a tiny bit late for work.'

'And if he doesn't turn you down, I get to be chief bridesmaid and dance under the fairy lights in that amazing barn?' Marcie asked.

Elle grinned. 'You most definitely do.'

'Good. I'm going back to my place. Pack your overnight bag,' Marcie said, and hugged her.

A fortnight without Elle.

It had felt like a year.

Longer than a year.

Charlie closed his eyes. He should've said yes. Then he could've managed here without her, simply counting down the days until Mike and Angie had found his replacement and he could move back to London with Elle. Now, he was counting endless days—and torturing himself with her ElleOfLondon social media accounts. He could've been sharing all those things with her, if he hadn't been so stupid and pushed her away. Cocktails in rooftop bars. Wisteria cascading down Chelsea walls. Geraniums in window-boxes. Swans and deckchairs in Green Park. Coffee in a trendy shop, perfectly styled in a double-walled glass. Street food and dancing on the banks of the Thames.

He didn't want to live in London any more;

but he was miserable at Bluebell Farm without her.

And finally he came to the conclusion that it was time to risk his heart again. Home was where Elle was. If he couldn't persuade her to come back to Bluebell Farm, then he'd move to London. Better to be with her, than to be without her.

But how did he persuade her to give him a chance? What would convince her that he meant it?

He could write his feelings on A3 cards and stand at her doorway, playing romantic music on his phone and getting her to read the cards one by one.

He could take her to a small theatre where he'd hired a singer-songwriter to play her a love song on a piano, under a spotlight.

He could sing to her himself—as he'd sort of done during milking. Say, The Beatles' 'Michelle', but switching her name into the song instead.

He could take her to a flashy restaurant to declare himself, or for afternoon tea in the glitziest hotel in London. Whisk her off to Paris, to Rome, to Venice.

But somehow an extravagant gesture didn't feel right. Not when he'd first fallen for a girl in a bluebell wood with a nightingale singing in the background.

Keep it simple, he decided. He went to see her parents and explained to them what he wanted to do, and they gave him their blessing along with her address. Then he caught the train to London. It felt very strange to be back in the city, the place that had held some of his darkest days as well as some of his happiest.

He still hadn't worked out what to say to Elle; but one thing he did know she liked was flowers. At Liverpool Street, he bought an armful of the prettiest flowers at the flower stand, then caught the Tube to the Oval. His heart was racing as he followed the directions on his phone to the mansion block where she lived.

The building was beautiful, a large Edwardian brick-and-slate building with white windows and balconies: exactly the sort of place he could imagine her living.

He pressed the intercom button and waited.

Elle wasn't expecting visitors. She hadn't made any arrangements to meet anyone, either.

It was probably someone door-knocking for a politician. She thought about ignoring it, but then the buzzer went again.

Whoever it was, they were persistent.

She rolled her eyes. She'd answer with a polite 'thank you, but no', and then get on with her packing. 'Tha—' she began.

'Elle. Can I come in?'

She recognised the voice instantly 'Charlie? What are you doing here?'

'I wanted to see you.'

'I'm on the ground floor. Turn right into the corridor, and I'm the second door on the right.'

Why did Charlie want to see her? And why was he in London, when he'd said he didn't want to be there any more?

When he knocked on the door, she opened it and he thrust a large bunch of flowers into her hands.

'Thank you—they're gorgeous,' she said.

'They're not great, but they're the best I could get at the station,' he said, looking apologetic.

'They're perfect. Even nicer than the ones you sent me last week.' She paused. 'Can I get you a coffee or something?'

'No. I just want to talk.' He gave her a wry smile. 'I don't think I've ever felt so nervous in my life.'

'Nervous?' she echoed, puzzled. Why on earth would Charlie be feeling nervous?

'Because I'm just about to...' He blew out a breath. 'This could be the best thing I've ever done, or the most stupid, and I have no idea which.'

'Come and sit down,' she said, and ushered him into the living room. 'I'll just put these flowers in water.'

* * *

The living room was as Charlie expected: pale walls, wooden flooring with a bright rug, a comfortable sofa, an armchair with a reading lamp and a large bookcase stuffed with books. There was a small table with four chairs, which he guessed doubled as her desk as well as her dining table; and prominent on the wall was Frieda's watercolour of Bluebell Farm. On the mantelpiece were framed photos of Elle on her graduation day with her parents, one of her parents at Bluebell Farm, and one of Elle with another woman he guessed might be her best friend.

She came back in. 'Are you sure you don't want anything to drink?'

'I just want to talk.' He shook his head. 'I've been trying to work out the right words, all the way here, and I can't find them. But a flashy gesture doesn't seem right, either. So what I'm saying now is unpolished, but it's honest. Straight from my heart.' He took a deep breath. 'You've been gone for two weeks. It feels like a lifetime. So I'm here to say I'm sorry I pushed you away. I love Bluebell Farm, but I hate being there without you. If being with you means being in London, then—even though I never wanted to come back—it's London all the way. Because you're here, and you're where my heart is.' And then, because he couldn't hold the words back any longer, he blurted out, 'I love you.'

She stared at him. He couldn't read her expression.

Was she pleased, horrified, indifferent?

All his wits seemed to have deserted him.

The time he'd thought crawled so slowly before was now setting a new world slowness record.

Or maybe he'd got this very badly wrong.

'I'm sorry,' he said. 'Now you're back in London, things must seem different. I'll go. Forget we had this conversation, because I don't want you to feel awkward with your parents. I'll make sure I stay out of your way, so it won't be cringey when you come home.' He stood up, ready to walk away and leave her to find what she really wanted from life.

Except she stood up, too. Took his hand. 'You love me. You want to be with me. Even if it means coming back to London,' she repeated.

He couldn't speak, just nodded.

'When you rang my doorbell, I was packing,' she said. 'I was coming back to Bluebell Farm to ask you to be with me. To say I'll come back to Norfolk if that's the only way we can be together.'

'But—what about your job? The one you worked so hard for?'

'It's not enough, if I don't have you,' she said. 'London isn't enough, either. I want you.'

She wanted him.

She'd been coming home to him, just as he'd been trying to come home to her.

It might still be a bit complicated but, together, he knew they'd find a way to work this out.

He wrapped his arms round her and kissed her lingeringly.

'I wasn't looking to fall in love,' he said. 'And opening my heart to love again and risking losing you scares me witless. But then I realised that being without you was way, way worse than living with the fear.' He stroked her face. 'That photo shoot for the wedding—that's when it hit me what I really wanted. You walking down the aisle to me with an armful of bluebells, our closest family and friends there to share the moment. It felt so right. I wanted it to be for real.'

'But you didn't even come over to review the photographs,' she protested.

'Because I was terrified that Frieda's lens might have captured how I really felt about you—and that you didn't feel the same way.' He took out his phone and showed her a photograph. 'Tell me what you see.'

'We're acting out a first dance.' She looked at

him. 'I was thinking about the night we danced together outside the shepherd's hut.'

'The night I kissed you for the first time, with the nightingale singing.' He nodded. 'I was remembering that, too. And thinking about how much I wanted to kiss you again, even though I knew you were leaving and it wouldn't be fair of me to hold you back.'

'I wanted to kiss you, too, but you'd told me we could only be friends. I thought it was better to stay in London and be miserable without you, than to see you every day and pine for you.'

'How stupid are we?' he asked. 'There has to be a way to make this work for both of us, Elle. I love you. I want to watch the seasons change at Bluebell Farm with you at my side—but I don't want you to sacrifice your job. I know how hard you've worked for your promotion.'

'My best friend suggested something today,' Elle said. 'Flexible working. Maybe I can work a couple of days a week in London, and the rest of the time in Norfolk.'

'That's it.' He stared at her. 'Why the hell didn't *we* think of that?'

'Because neither of us has been in a good place,' she said. 'You're still healing from losing Jess.'

'I'll always miss her and I'll always love her,' Charlie said. 'But the thing is, love isn't like a cake that gets scoffed and then there's nothing left. It's something that grows and changes. And I'm finally ready to move on—with you.' He paused. 'But what about you and the Mr Wrongs?'

She nodded. 'I was thinking of all the men who'd let me down, and panicking that if things went wrong between us it would make life difficult for Mum and Dad. Using my work as a barrier between us meant that I could be a coward and not have to take the risk. Except I've really missed you, Charlie. And although I love the bright lights and the glitter of London, it's all felt a bit pointless without you. I don't feel connected, the way I used to. I want my job—but I want you more.'

'What if your manager says you need to stay in London?'

'Then we tweak my five-year plan and I set up my own consultancy a little bit early.' She dragged in a breath. 'Which is a bit scary.'

'I've got your back,' he said. 'Whatever support you need, it's yours. Anything from building you the office of your dreams through to helping you stuff promotional goody bags at three in the morning.'

'I'll hold you to that,' she said. 'And I've got your back, too. Everything from teaching you all the wildflower stuff for your nature walks through to bringing your lunch when you're busy foxproofing the hen house.'

'I'll hold you to that,' he echoed.

'And we need a new five-year plan. A joint one.'

'A flexible one,' he added. 'Starting with seeing if your boss agrees to changing the way you work. The main thing is that you're happy.'

'That we're *both* happy,' she corrected.

'And next on the list is to take our time. Much as I'd love to sweep you off your feet, ask you to marry me and then be the first couple married in the barn, that wouldn't be fair. I want you to be sure that life at Bluebell Farm is enough for you,' he said. 'If it's not, we'll do a re-think. We'll tweak things until it works for both of us.'

'That's fair,' she said. 'Though I'm pretty sure my feelings aren't going to change.' She reached up to kiss him. 'I love you too, Charlie. And you've missed the last train back. Can you bear a night in London?'

'With you,' he said, 'I think I can.'

EPILOGUE

Four months later

'I KNOW YOU'RE BUSY, but breakfast is the most important meal of the day,' Charlie said, leaning against the jamb of the door of Elle's office in the farmhouse.

Elle sniffed the air. 'Is that croissants I smell?'

'You'll have to come with me to find out.' He held out a hand. 'Half an hour's break. Most people aren't even at their desk yet.'

'I am, because I'm a morning person,' Elle said. 'Which is just as well, since you're up a mad o'clock to do the milking.'

'Indeed.' He smiled as she saved her file, closed her laptop and went to join him.

'Are Mum and Dad in the kitchen?'

'No idea. We're not eating here.'

She frowned. 'Why didn't you just text me from the cottage and tell me you had croissants?'

'Because we're not eating there, either.' H

picked up the wicker basket he'd stashed in the hallway. 'We're eating al fresco.' He stole a kiss. 'I did think about blindfolding you, but I didn't want anyone getting the wrong idea.'

She kissed him back. 'Indeed. So is there any particular reason for breakfast outdoors?'

'I just thought it would be nice.'

She gave him a sidelong look. 'In four months of living with you, I've learned there's always a reason why you do something.'

He just laughed. 'Stop being so suspicious.'

She realised that they were heading towards the wildflower meadow. As they got closer, she saw that he'd set out a table and two chairs. The table was neatly set for two with a damask tablecloth and napkins, plus a milk jug containing a froth of meadowsweet.

'This definitely looks like a special occasion,' she said, letting him seat her.

'It's a Wednesday, the weather's nice, and you're here. That's special enough for me. Can't a man try to do something romantic for his girlfriend, once in a while?' He opened the wicker basket, took out a flask and a stainless steel bottle, and poured them both some coffee, adding milk to hers.

'Thank you.' She smiled. 'Actually, this is lovely. There must be a gazillion birds in that meadow, singing their heads off and scoffing all the seed. Just as I'm going to be scoffing croissants in a moment, right?'

He rolled his eyes and took a dish of butter and a pot of raspberry jam from the basket, swiftly followed by a box containing croissants wrapped in a linen napkin. 'As you demand, princess.'

'And they're still warm. You are a prince among men,' Elle declared.

'No regrets about moving back?' he asked, taking a croissant and buttering it.

'No. I can do most of my job from here, with a Tuesday catch-up in the London office and the occasional client visit. I still get the buzz of London, and I get the cows and the sheep and the chickens and all this gorgeousness six days a week.' She grinned. 'And, best of all, I get to wake up with you every morning—which is worth putting up with the stroppy magpies yelling their heads off.'

'Good,' he said.

'No regrets about asking me to move in with you?' she asked.

'I get to wake up every morning with the woman I love, even though she hogs the duvet and the pillows and she warms her cold feet on me,' he said. 'Nope. No regrets. But I do want to propose…'

Elle's heartbeat bumped up a notch.

'…a tweak to the five-year plan,' he said.

'I'm listening,' she said.

'Four months ago, I did something very stupid. I walked by this meadow, and I told someone to go back to London without me. I propose to change that.'

She frowned. 'We already changed it. You came after me—on exactly the same day I decided to come back for you.'

'The thing with communications specialists is that they never stop talking,' Charlie said. 'Even more than the hens.'

'Oi. That's cheeky,' she protested.

He coughed. 'I was going to wait until the first bluebells, next year. Except I can't. So I'm going to ask you now.' He dropped to one knee beside her. 'Elle Newton, I love you very much. I want to make a family with you, and I want to make that family here, where your ancestors have farmed for decades. Though, if you really want to move back to London,' he added, 'I know now I'll do it for you, because being with you is more important to me than anything else in the world. Will you marry me?'

He took a box from his pocket and opened it. Nestled among the velvet was the *moi-et-toi* ring she'd described to him on the beach, the day that they'd taken the fake engagement pictures for the farm. A narrow band of platinum, with a pink sapphire heart nestled next to a tanzanite, the colour of the bluebells in the wood and of Charlie's eyes.

Charlie paid attention. He noticed. He remembered.

And she knew they were going to have a good and happy life together.

'Charlie Webb, you're the love of my life,' she said. 'Yes, I'll marry you and make a family with you, too. Here. Because you've made this place home for me again.'

He slid the ring onto her finger, and kissed her. 'And in the spring,' he said, 'I want you to walk down the aisle of the barn to me, carrying a posy of bluebells. Except this time it's going to be for real. And for ever.'

'That,' she said, 'sounds perfect.'

* * * * *

If you enjoyed this story, check out these other great reads from Kate Hardy

Crowning His Secret Princess
One Week in Venice with the CEO
Snowbound with the Brooding Billionaire
Surprise Heir for the Princess

All available now!